Hail Mary

Beverly Sade

Hail Mary is a work of fiction. Names, characters, places, and incidents either are the product of the author's imagination or are used fictitiously. Any resemblance to actual persons, living or dead, events, or locales is entirely coincidental.

ISBN-13: 978-0692703618
ISBN-10: 0692703616

Beverly **S**ade **P**ublications

DEDICATION

For Tylin, my heartbeat…everything I do is for you.

CONTENTS

CHAPTER ONE

As I lay still on the doctor's table, my mind ran wild. I could tell by the dismaying expression on Dr. Watts face he would be delivering bad news yet again. "Okay, let me get you all cleaned up here," he said. He grabbed a paper towel and wiped my belly clean. *Here we go again with this shit*, I thought to myself. "I'm afraid you've had another chemical pregnancy," Dr. Watts said. "Maryana, I'm sorry. This doesn't mean that you won't ever…"

"I know doctor, I can try again and blah blah blah, please spare me. I've heard this way too many times before," I said, cutting him off. Tears began to well up in my eyes and I just needed to get out of there. I didn't mean to be rude but I'm sure he could understand my pain and frustration. This was my fourth miscarriage within two years. I had nine total. The one thing my husband wanted more than anything in the world, I was unable to give to him. I reached into my Celine bag and grabbed my oversized Versace sunglasses and scurried out of Dr. Watts's office.

"Excuse me, Mrs. Mendez!" the secretary called out. "Dr. Watts would like to schedule you for a follow up." I kept walking. "I'll give you a call to schedule an appointment," I said, as I walked out. This was just too much. I jumped into my car and sped down Palm Avenue. How was I going to explain to my husband that I lost another baby? *He's going to think it's my fault. Well, maybe I shouldn't tell him right away. Things have been going so good with us. I don't want to ruin it*, I thought to myself.

You see, my husband Andre and I were together for all of my adult life. I was only twenty-one and had just graduated from UCLA when we met. I guess you can say it was sort of love at first sight. Well, until he opened his mouth. I couldn't stand him. I thought he was so arrogant. I remember our first date when I called him out on it. He looked at me with the most alluring smile and said, "Baby don't confuse my confidence with arrogance." I just looked at him and shook my head. He was something else. I don't know how he did it but he persuaded me into a second date. Maybe it was the fact he was fine as hell, 6'2, chocolate skin, pretty teeth and worked out religiously or that I never dated someone so young but so sure of where they were going in life. At only twenty-five, he was working for one of the top advertising firms in Lakeside, California. That was impressive considering he came from a wealthy family but still, he was determined to make his own way. Me on the other hand, I had no choice but to find my own way.

I grew up in Queens, New York. South Jamaica, Queens to be exact. I lived in a small run-down apartment with my older sister Ashton and my mother Sheila. Stepping over junkies, beer bottles and soiled diapers before entering our building was the norm. Oh gosh, and the hallways; they reeked of stale cigarette smoke and urine. I woke up every morning thinking, *this can't be life*. Every time my mother got a new boyfriend she would say, "Girls this is it, we won't be here much longer. We're getting the hell out of this place." That line soon grew tired. She would change men like she changed clothes. I guess she was looking for someone to save us. Problem was, she had bad taste in men. I mean, she always picked the bad ones. She named me after my father Martino Mendez. Hell, I never understood why she gave me his last name. I never even met him. In spite of him being married to another woman, my mother was in love with him and she believed he was in love with her. She told me how he provided for her and my sister, even had them leaving in a fancy apartment in Forest Hills. She played the role of his side chick for two years but as soon as she got pregnant with me everything changed. He said he didn't want to ruin his family. When my mother refused to get an abortion, he cut all ties.

I wish I could paint this picture of her being a strong, single mother who worked hard to provide for her children but I'm not here to sell you bullshit. Truth is, my mother didn't have a hustler bone in her body. With no job and no savings, she relied on government assistance to get by. I never understood how someone so beautiful and so charming could just settle for this kind of life. I hated my surroundings but I knew it wasn't my last stop. Ashton told me, "Girl you gon' be something watch." She said that a lot and I believed her too. She was always cheering me on and supporting me in everything I did. Although she was only two years older than me, I looked at her like more of a mother figure. I always felt safe when she was around. Growing up my sister got in trouble a lot. She got suspended from school for fighting on the regular. I lost count of how many times she was arrested for boosting. It was because of her I went to school fly every day. She kept me laced in Gucci, Fendi and Prada. Nobody understood Ashton like me. Everyone in my family thought she was crazy. Even my grandmother would say, "Something is wrong with that damn child, she's sick in the head!" After a while, my mother couldn't ignore her aggressive behavior and abrupt mood swings. My sister began seeing a psychiatrist when she was seventeen and was diagnosed with bipolar disorder. My mother saw this as the perfect opportunity to collect a social security check.

On June 21, 2004, I graduated from Newtown High School with a 4.0 GPA. I stood at the podium proud, receiving a standing ovation after delivering my valedictorian speech. My mother sat in the audience with my grandmother, smiling and taking pictures. I was surprised my sister didn't show, especially since she was so excited for my big day.

"Mom, where's Ashton?" I asked.

"I don't know. She said she was coming."

"Did you try calling her?"

"Call her for what? She's a grown damn woman."

"And I know that's right," my grandmother chimed in. I sucked my teeth at the both of them and reached into my bag for my cellphone. I called Ashton repeatedly and didn't get an answer.

"I'm gonna go home. I need to make sure she's okay."

"I'm sure she's fine. She probably done ran off with some lil' boy," my grandmother replied. "Everybody is waiting on you Mary. You can't be late to your own party."

"I don't care. I need to make sure my sister is okay. Unlike you two, I do care about her," I spat.

I felt uneasy the entire train ride home. I had that feeling like something wasn't right. I ran to our building, through the pissy hallways and up three flights of stairs in four-inch stiletto heels. I turned the key into the lock, with my hands sweating and my heart racing.

"Ashton!" I shouted. "Ashton!" I walked through the living room and into the kitchen. I checked all of our bedrooms and there was no sign of her. I started to think, *maybe they're right. Maybe she got caught up with a guy or something.* Then I walked into the bathroom and there she was, lying in a tub full of bloody water. "Oh my god, oh my god, oh my god...Ashton no! What did you do?" I nearly fell in the tub trying to lift her stiff body. Both of her arms were cut from her wrist to her elbows. A prescription bottle lay empty on the floor, along with a note that read...

Mary,

I'm sorry. I tried to hang on for you but hanging on is just too much to bare. Please don't hate me. I love you more than you'll ever know. See you next lifetime little sis.

Love Always,

Ash

That's it. That's all she wrote. I couldn't stop crying. I had never cried so hard in my life.

"911 what's the address of the emergency?"

"106-67 160th Street, in Queens, New York. My sister she uh, she took pills and cut her wrist. There's so much blood," I sobbed.

"Okay. Are you there alone?" the operator asked.

"Yes, it's just me and my sister. Please hurry," I said.

"What is your name?" she quizzed.

"Maryana. Maryana Mendez."

Ashton was pronounced dead shortly after the police and paramedics arrived. She was just nineteen years old. To this day I blame my mother for what happened to my sister. If it weren't for those damn antidepressants she practically forced down Ashton's throat, she would still be alive.

I stuck to my plans and got as far away from home as possible. I was accepted into UCLA's Communications Studies program. Luckily for me, I received a partial scholarship and financial aid covered the rest of my expenses. I also took advantage of campus living. I would've been a fool not to. Rent was expensive and I wasn't about to end up in somebody's club, pole dancing for a living. Living in Los Angeles was like a breath of fresh air. I was only eighteen years old but desperately felt the need to start over. It felt good being in a place where I didn't know anyone. It was exactly what I needed.

After graduation I moved to Spring Valley, California, which is right outside of San Diego. My best friend Bree and I found a cute two bedroom apartment. I met Bree my freshman year in college. She and I were two peas in a pod. People asked if we were sisters so much till we started telling everyone we were. Funny story how we met. I walked into the bathroom on campus and there she was, on the phone going in on her boyfriend.

"You didn't think I would find out? You ain't shit! I'm done with your ass!" Bree immediately burst into tears as soon as she hung up the phone.

"Are you okay?" I asked.

"No, I just found out my boyfriend was cheating on me. Then he has the nerve to be running around with this dusty ass bitch that's not even on my level," Bree said.

"Girl please, the side bitch is always a mess," I said, rolling my eyes. "How did you find out about her?"

"She posted pictures of them together on Instagram."

"Oh, hell no. He need his ass whooped for even letting another chick disrespect you like that. I mean, damn, it's rules to being a sideline hoe." We both looked at each other and laughed.

"I can't believe I wasted a whole year on his broke ass."

"Broke? And he's cheating? Girl look in that mirror. You can do better," I said. "Fuck him."

"Yeah, you're right. Fuck him. Time to move on to bigger and better things," she said.

"Exactly!" I cosigned. "Where are you from? You don't talk like these Cali girls."

"I'm from Philly!" she said, proudly.

"I'm from Queens."

As we were walking out of the bathroom she said, "Oh I almost forgot. I'm Brielle, but you can call me Bree." And just like that we became friends and from that day forward we were joined at the hip.

To my surprise I got a job in my field fast. Well, not necessarily a paying job. I worked as an intern at FOX channel 5 news in San Diego and although I wasn't getting paid, I was more than grateful for the opportunity. I was confident that with my beauty, charming personality and communications degree, I would be on the air in no time. Besides, I was in with the head people in charge. Everyone around the office loved me. I also worked nights as a server at an upscale restaurant and lounge downtown. This is where I met Andre.

From the start we were drawn to each other. I've never used the word beautiful to describe a man before, but to me that's what he was. When he smiled at me, he had me right then and there. Yes, he got on my nerves once he opened his mouth but damn this boy was fine! I wanted to just slap the shit out of him for being so cocky, then take him home and fuck him all night long. But you know, I couldn't go out like that. I mean, not on the first date. He would have to work for it…and that's exactly what he did.

He went out of his way to make me feel special. He wined and dined me regularly, bought me flowers and expensive gifts. He definitely knew how to treat a girl. What I liked most about him was that we connected on a deeper level. Although we came from two different worlds, we understood each other. Our conversations were always stimulating. We could talk for hours about any and everything. I opened up to him about my upbringing and things that I've gone through. He told me as long as he was around I wouldn't have to worry about a thing. He said, "Baby from here on out, I gotchu."

Six months later, I moved into Andre's penthouse. It was a major upgrade from the small two bedroom apartment I shared with Bree. It had four bedrooms, four full bathrooms, a bulthaup kitchen, and a step-up dining room that opened onto a private terrace. There was a top-floor master suite, with his and hers closets and a spa-like tub in every bathroom.

Andre proposed to me that year on New Year's Eve. He got down on one knee in the freezing cold and in the middle of Times Square. When he revealed the 3.5-carat cushion-cut diamond Tacori ring I nearly fainted. "Of course I'll marry you!" I shouted. "I had a feeling you would say that," he said, jokingly. We laughed and then kissed passionately. I loved him and there was no doubt in my mind I wanted to spend the rest of my life with him.

Everyone said we were moving too fast and that we should slow down. When I say everyone, I mean Andre's family. They told him he needed to get to know me better and that there was no need to rush into marriage. He wasn't trying to hear it and neither was I. We said fuck everyone and ran off to Vegas and got married. I didn't see the point in exchanging vows in front of people who didn't want to see us married in the first place. I didn't care about a fancy white dress or the big, glitzy fairy tale wedding. It was about us and our union. That was all that mattered to me.

Three years later, Andre left the advertising firm and opened his own consulting firm. I put my dreams of becoming a news anchor to the side and devoted all of my time to my husband. I worked as his executive assistant and together we built a multi-million dollar firm, Global Consulting. He was a marketing genius and was considered the go to guy, offering services to government agencies, such as the military and the Internal Revenue Service. He also handled public relations for recording artist, athletes and members of the political elite. You may have even downloaded one of his million dollar apps to your cellphone. To sum it up, my husband was the shit and in my eyes there was no one greater.

Global Consulting only became more successful. We were seeing the kind of money that never sleeps. At now twenty-seven and my husband thirty-one, we had more than I could've ever imagined. We purchased a 6.5 million dollar mansion, 7 bedrooms, 7.5 baths, 10 car garage, 14,710 square feet, which sat on 2.98 acres of land. Andre and I hosted lavish parties at our home regularly. Everything we did was big. We were living the good life. One that only the most prestigious could afford. I always thought once my husband's business took off I would get back to me. You know, get my Mary Jane Paul on. I was still holding on to my dream of being a successful TV news anchor, but Andre wasn't having it. He didn't want me working. He wouldn't even let me help out at the office anymore. "No wife of mines is going to punch the clock every day," he told me. He was very adamant about it. "Just concentrate on giving me some babies, that's all I need you to do," he said. I wanted that too. I planned on giving him lots of babies...but that was easier said than done.

CHAPTER TWO

The problem wasn't conceiving. I'd been pregnant by my husband more times than I would like to remember. I miscarried each and every time. In the beginning, I was told by doctors that miscarriages were very common in the first twelve weeks and that more than likely I would conceive again and have a healthy baby. Our close family and friends would say, "You're so young. You have plenty of time. It's going to happen." But after four years of trying, I wasn't so sure they were right. We tried numerous fertility treatments, they all failed. Our last hope was In Vitro Fertilization. I started seeing Dr. Watts about six months ago and after three cycles of treatment, I conceived. Andre didn't want to get his hopes up. He didn't go to any of my doctor appointments and he never even talked about the pregnancy. In my heart, I felt like this time would be different. I never carried past ten weeks, so at three months I thought we were in the clear.

When Dr. Watts told me I lost the baby I was devastated. I didn't know how to tell my husband the bad news. I was almost ashamed to tell Andre. I never told him or anyone how I truly felt about not being able to give him a child, but deep down inside it made me feel like I was less of a woman.

I'm curled up in bed, with my cellphone turned off and watching reruns of Scandal on Netflix when Andre walks in.

"Hey baby. I left the office as soon as I seen your text, "Are you okay?"

"No, I'm not okay. I called you several times. Why weren't you answering my calls?" I asked.

"Thanks to this damn new assistant, my meetings ran back to back," he said, removing his suit jacket and undoing his tie. "I called you not too long ago and I kept getting your voicemail, so I rushed over," he explained.

"I found out today I had a miscarriage," I said in a low, sad voice.

"C'mon Mary not again," he murmured.

"What did you just say?" I asked, hoping he hadn't said what I thought he did.

"I said, not again," he replied. "What?"

I shook my head at him. "Unbelievable. You think this is my fault, don't you?" I asked, staring him down.

"That's not what I meant. Of course I don't think it's your fault. I just think it's time that we accept this for what it is."

"And what exactly is that?"

"You weren't able to get pregnant on your own. These damn UVF treatments aren't working…"

"It's IVF," I interrupted.

"Whatever it is. It's not working. We're not able to have children Mary."

"No, I'm not able to. You can go out there and have as many as you want. You're perfectly fine. I'm the one with the problem," I sobbed.

"Look at me." He put his index finger under my chin to lift my head. "I'm sorry, I didn't mean to come off so insensitive. I love you and this is our problem. We're in this together," he said, in a soothing voice. We'll figure this out."

"So does that mean you're open to adoption now?" He stood there giving me this look like, *oh boy, here we go.*

"Baby, I'll think about it," he said.

"Okay, I'll take that," I replied. "That's better than a no."

He wrapped his arms around me and held me tight. He whispered in my ear, "Everything is going to be alright." And just like that he was able to put my mind and heart at ease. Whenever I was in his arms I felt secure and protected…like I didn't have a worry in the world. I know this may sound pathetic, but I couldn't imagine what life would be like without him. Bree always thought I leaned on my husband more than I should. She always told me I needed to step out of Andre's shadows. I know that she meant well but she didn't understand. She didn't know what it was like for me growing up. I came from nothing and sometimes I feel like I came from no one. It's been six years since I last seen my mother. When I left for college I checked in with her periodically. Not that I wanted to but because my grandmother was always feeding me a bunch of "she's still your mother" crap, but after she died, so did all communication between my mother and I. So yes, maybe I did rely on my husband for all of my emotional support but that's because he was all I had. He was my lover, my best friend, and my confidant. He was my everything.

Over the next few weeks, Andre and I spent a lot of time apart. He was away on business a lot, working to close a few deals. We also had a big charity gala coming up, so his hands were full preparing for that as well. I didn't complain whenever he had to go. I was good at giving him space to handle business. I was never the nagging, insecure type. After a long hectic day of work, I wanted to give him peace of mind. I made sure that our home was his safe haven.

The day before Andre returned from his business trip, Bree and I met up for a little pampering and shopping. Andre and I hadn't been intimate since the miscarriage and after three weeks, I was more than ready to put it on him.

"Andre is going to love you in that Vicky's set you just bought," Bree said.

"Girl it's going down on sight," I giggled. "As soon as he walks through the door."

"Horny ass. Always got dick on the brain."

"Whatever, I guess you've rubbed off on me." We both laughed and continued to walk through Fashion Valley Mall. "C'mon girl, let's go in Barneys," I said. "Oh, so fill me in on the new guy."

"Ugh! His ass is cut already," she said with her face twisted in annoyance.

"What...whyyy? I thought you liked him."

"I did but now he's showing his true colors. He's just too damn clingy for me," Bree said.

"Excuse me, can I see these both in a size 38 please," I said to the shoe salesman. I turned my attention back to Bree. "What do you mean?"

"He's been texting and calling too much. Always wanting to see me. Just getting on my nerves."

"He likes you. What would you rather him do? Not call or text or ever bother to see you?"

"Mary, you know I'm easily turned off."

"Poor guy," I laughed. "Somebody should've warned him, you're a man eater."

"Whatever bitch, I'm not a man eater. I just don't like em' thirsty," she said.

She was always finding something she didn't like in a man. After a few failed relationships I think she developed major trust issues and was afraid to let another man in. I jokingly told her once, I would probably look out of my window and see it snowing in San Diego before I would see her settle down with someone.

"Did you ladies find everything okay?" the blonde cashier asked.

"Yes we did, thank you," I replied.

"Wonderful," she said. "Your total comes to 6,751.89."

I pulled my black card and driver's license out of my wallet and handed it to her. "Here you go."

"Thanks so much for the shoes and bag. One of these days, I'll be able to take you shopping!" Bree said.

"You're welcome boo and I know you will!"

"Yup, just as soon as I find me a sugar daddy," she said, giggling.

I smiled and shook my head at her. "I can't deal. You play too much."

Bree flipped her long, 24 inch weave. "Bitch, "I'm dead serious."

"And that's the sad part," I said. We both laughed. "Oh, I almost forgot. Are you coming to the charity event next week?"

"Yes, I'll be there."

"You just might get lucky and find your sugar daddy there," I said, jokingly.

"I'm counting on it girl," she said, laughing.

The Next Day...8:00 p.m.

The moment Andre walked through the door he could see the mood was already set. There were rose petals at the door, leading up to the staircase. All the lights were off and there were lit candles all over. "Baby!" he shouted. "I get filthy when that liquor get into me. I've been thinking, I've been thinking. Why can't I keep my fingers off it, baby? I want you, na na." I turned Beyonce's "Drunk in Love" up even louder when I heard him call out for me. I met him at the staircase, wearing sexy lingerie and six-inch Christian Louboutin heels. I was also wearing a garter belt that was attached to my thigh-high stockings. That always drove him wild.

"Hey daddy," I said, seductively.

"Hey baby," he said, staring me down as if I was a piece of meat.

"Did you miss me?"

"Hell yeah. You know I missed you." He put his hands around my waist and pulled me in closer to him. "Sexy ass," he whispered. I stuck my tongue in his mouth and kissed him passionately.

"Show me how much you miss me," I said, as I turned and walked away from him, switching my hips. He followed me into our bedroom, unbuttoning his shirt. I took another sip of ciroc and placed my glass on the dresser. I walked over to him, then dropped to my knees and started undoing his pants. His dick was hard as a rock. I took all ten inches into my mouth and down my throat. He threw his head back and moaned in ecstasy. "Damn girl," he murmured. The louder he moaned, the harder I sucked. Andre carried me over to the bed and slid my panties off. He spread my legs wide open and dived into my pussy. He took two fingers and pumped in and out of me, as his tongue swirled around my clit. "I'm about to cum," I shouted. "C'mon," he replied, still licking me. He sucked all of my juices and I squirmed uncontrollably. He grabbed my hips and entered me, making me scream in pleasure. We switched positions. He always loved me on top. He cupped my breast and squeezed hard, as I bounced up and down on his dick. "Ahh Shit!" he yelled. "Yeah, just like that," he said, smacking me on my ass. He gripped my cheeks and pumped harder and faster, until we climaxed simultaneously. I curled up next to him, resting my head on his chest. He held me tight and ran his fingers through my hair, until I fell asleep in his arms.

The next morning I woke up on cloud nine. I know what you're thinking, and no, it had nothing to do with Andre banging my back out the night before. I received a follow up email from Michael, my old boss at the news station. Michael and I always had a good relationship. He took a chance on me when I was fresh out of college and had zero experience. Thanks to him, I went from an intern to a field reporter in less than ninety days. Andre didn't know this, but I called Michael when he was away. Our conversation went so well that he invited me down to the station to talk in person. It wasn't a sit-down formal interview or anything like that. We just kind of hung out around the office and did some catching up. I knew he wanted to see me in person first to make sure that I hadn't fell off. I knew that by the way his eyes lit up when he saw me, "Looking good, Maryana. You still got it darling!" he said, in his flamboyant voice. I told him how badly I wanted to get back into the work field. Michael knew how passionate I was about news broadcasting, and he always felt as though I had the potential to be the next dateline news star. So, when I received the email from him stating he would like to bring me in for an interview with the hiring managers, I was more than thrilled. Only problem was, I would have to find a way to break the news to my husband and I knew that wouldn't be an easy task.

CHAPTER THREE

"**O**n behalf of Global Consulting, I want to thank you all for your generous donations tonight. As my husband mentioned earlier, over 500,000 people in the United States live with Multiple Sclerosis. However, there are many misconceptions about this disease and each and every one of you have played a significant role in bringing awareness and supporting a good cause. The funds we raised here tonight will support research, programs and services for people affected by MS. So again, thank you." I stood there confidently, delivering my speech and looking good while doing it, in my Balmain dress and Giuseppe heels. "Now that we're done with business, let's get this party started!" I said, in a playful voice.

Hosting was my thing. I was much better at it than Andre. I loved public speaking, entertaining guest and being the life of the party. I was the outgoing one. Andre was more reserved at functions like this, maybe even a little boring at times. But it was okay, I had enough spunk for the both of us.

As Andre and I worked the room, greeting guest, I noticed an unfamiliar face staring back at me. At first I thought it was nothing. *Maybe she's admiring my outfit*, I thought to myself. But no, that wasn't it. In a room full of smiling faces, she stuck out like a sore thumb. She was upset and I got the feeling that whatever it was that had her so bothered, it involved me.

I ditched Andre so I could have a chance to speak with her. I didn't know what I was going to say or how I was going to say it. I kept my eyes on her, as I made my way through the crowded room.

"There you are. Where are you off to in such a hurry?" Mrs. Blanchard asked. Mrs. Blanchard worked for city council and was responsible for the Marina District, in San Diego. She was well connected and was always one of our biggest contributors whenever we had any kind of charity event.

"Oh, hi Mrs. Blanchard. How are you?" I asked, as I hugged her.

"I'm doing good and yourself?"

"I'm good. Everything's good," I said, looking out into the crowd, hoping that the mystery woman was still in my sight.

"I can see that. You look absolutely stunning!"

"Thank you. I'm sorry, I don't mean to be in a hurry but I have to return a very important call."

"No apologies necessary. Go take care of your business. I'll catch up with you later," she replied.

My eyes skimmed the room but there was no sign of the mystery woman. I scurried out of the ballroom and out to the hallway, but it was clear. *Dammit! Where the hell did she go?* Before giving up, I made one last desperate attempt to find her in the ladies room, but still no sign of her. It left me feeling perplexed and uneasy. Still, I returned to the gala with my poker face on. I didn't want Andre, or our guest to suspect something was wrong.

"Something weird just happened," I said to Bree.

"What happened?" she asked, with her face wearing a look of concern.

"There was this woman here, just staring me down. It was weird. She..."

"What do you mean staring you down?" Bree interrupted.

"You know when you catch someone staring at you, they quickly turn the other way?"

"Yeah."

"Well, she didn't. She kept staring. I think she wanted me to see her."

"What did she look like?

"Gorgeous," I said. "Like a young, Halle Berry."

"Well, Ms. Berry better chill before she get her ass whooped," Bree said, half-jokingly.

"I'm telling you Bree. There was something up with this woman. Before I could even approach her she was gone!"

"Wow that's crazy," she replied.

Bree signaled with her eyes that someone was behind me. I turned around and it was Andre.

"Excuse me beautiful. Would you like to dance?"

"I don't think my husband would like that," I said, smiling.

"I won't tell if you won't tell," he chuckled.

He put his hands on my waist and pulled me in close to him. John Legend's "All of me" played as we danced. "You're so beautiful," Andre said, as he stared deep into my eyes. "I just want you to know that I appreciate everything you do for me. I don't know what I'd do without you baby."

"And you'll never have to find out. I'm not going anywhere," I said. I wrapped my arms around his neck and kissed his lips. In the back of my mind, I wondered if Andre had any connection to the woman I'd seen. It was just something about her. I had this strange feeling like we had something in common. But whatever it was, if it was even anything at all, I knew eventually it would come to light.

After six years of marriage, Andre never stopped courting me. I know six years is not a very long time but let's be real, there are men who get married and after only six months the romantic courtship is over. But not with us. When we first met he told me, "I'll never stop trying to win you, even after you're mine." So, it was no surprise when Andre woke me up one morning and asked me if I was in the mood for a seven hour flight to Anguilla. He was spontaneous like that, it's what I loved most about him.

We arrived at the airport early in the afternoon, boarded our private jet and took off. We were only an hour into our flight and he was already lifting my skirt and removing my panties. Yes, we were members of the mile high club. I could go on and on about our many sex escapades, while in the air. There was nothing like it.

Anguilla was the perfect getaway. We rented a thirty-thousand dollar a night villa on a secluded beach, in Little Harbor. Andre and I both loved water activities, so usually we would be out, getting into everything. Snorkeling, scuba diving, jet-skiing, you name it. But this trip in particular, we didn't do much of anything. We mostly laid out on the beach, enjoying the beautiful scenery and the sounds of the waves.

"You're always naked." Andre said, smiling at me. I was topless and wearing nothing but a thong.

I rolled over on my back, put my hands behind my head and turned to him and said, "You know what they say, if you got it, flaunt it." He just laughed.

Andre and I got word of a private island, the people of Anguilla nicknamed "Paradise." We took a private Anguilla charter to Sandy Island. When we arrived I was lost in amazement. I could see why they called it Paradise. It was unlike any place I'd ever been before. It was so beautiful, so serene. It was just what Andre needed. He was always consumed with work, so whenever we got away, he liked to really get away. No cellphones, no laptops, just us. Well, we weren't exactly alone. Andre hired a personal concierge and a full staff to assist with cooking and cleaning. That was my husband, always doing it big. He worked hard but he played even harder. People close to us always said he was over the top with his spending. But hell, I didn't see anything wrong with it. Maybe it's because I was an even bigger spender than he was. I grew accustomed to living in a mansion, driving exotic cars and being able to drop ten to twenty thousand on designer clothes, bags and shoes whenever I desired. I can honestly say I was addicted the life we lived.

After five days, we returned back to San Diego. I didn't want to leave so soon but as usual, Andre had important business to take care of. He flew to New York City to negotiate a few million dollar deals.

Sometimes I wished he'd take me with him. I missed working at Global Consulting and being right in the mix of things. Still, being a housewife was important to me. I didn't have a problem with holding down the fort, while my husband went away to take care of business. At the same time, a part of me yearned for a professional life of my own. When Andre and I first met, I was miss independent. So independent that I didn't even change my last name when we got married. But now, I didn't even know who I was outside of being Andre's wife.

It was around 12:00 a.m. when my phone rang. I rolled over half sleep, picked up the phone and saw that it was a private number.

"Hello," I answered. There was silence on the other end of the phone. "Hello!" I said, raising my voice. Still no response. I hung up. Not even a minute later, my phone is ringing again. I rolled my eyes in the back of my head. "Hello," I said in a monotone voice. The caller still didn't say anything. I just hung up. They called once more, but I didn't answer. I put my phone on silent, rolled over and went to sleep.

The next morning I went to the gym, then met up with Bree for lunch. I hadn't seen her since the charity event and we hadn't talked much on the phone either, so I was really looking forward to catching up with my girl.

"Can I get you two another drink?" the blonde waitress asked.

"I'll have another cosmopolitan," I said.

"I'll have the same," Bree added.

"Okay, I'll be right back with your drinks," the waitress said, pleasantly.

"Enough about me and my drama. What's been going on with you?" Bree asked, as she dug her fork into her pasta.

"Lately I've been thinking a lot about going back to work."

"At Global Consulting?"

"Yeah, right. Even if I wanted to, Andre wouldn't allow it."

"Yeah, I know but why? Why doesn't he want you at the office? What does he have to hide?"

"I don't think it's a matter of him having something to hide. He just doesn't want me working," I said. "But girl, I'm just over it. I want to have my own shit going, you know?"

"I completely understand. I've been telling you that for the longest."

"Do you think it's too late?"

"Don't be silly. It's never too late and with your connections, you could be on the air, like that!" Bree said, snapping her finger.

"I'm going to let Andre know how I feel."

"Good," she said, taking a sip of what was left of her cocktail.

The waitress returned with our third round of drinks. I waited for her to walk away before I picked up where we left off.

"In other news," I said, sighing deeply. "Someone's been calling me from a private number."

"Saying what?" Bree asked.

"They're not saying anything. Just holding the phone."

"Who do you think it is?" she quizzed.

"Your guess is as good as mines," I said.

"Do you think it has anything to do with Andre?" she speculated.

"Why would I think that?"

"Look, I'm just saying. Usually these kind of calls can only mean one of two things. One, the man you're sleeping with woman is calling you, or the side chick sleeping with your man is calling you. And since I know you're not creeping, that means Andre definitely is," she said with certainty.

"Bree, we don't know that for sure," I debated.

"I've dated single men who were players and I've dated married men who play like they're single," she lectured. "I know the game."

"And you're saying I don't?"

"I'm saying you're not out here like I am, you've been with one man for the past seven years."

"Still, I'm no fool," I said, before tossing my drink down. "I would know if Andre were cheating on me. A woman's intuition never lies."

CHAPTER FOUR

Andre is sitting in his plush office, dressed to kill as always, in his Tom Ford suit. Just as he is preparing to leave for the day, his phone rings.

"Yes," he answered.

"Mr. Derou, I have Mr. Brockhoff on the line," Andre's secretary said.

"Brockhoff?" he asked, inquisitively.

"Yes, from Lawson and Associates," she replied.

"A real pain in my ass," he murmured.

She giggled on the other end of the phone. "Should I tell him you're not here sir?"

"Tell him I'm in a meeting," he said, coaching her to lie for him.

"Yes, of course."

He grabbed his cellphone, car keys, brief case and headed out the door. He walked through the long corridor, leaving the fragrance of his Versace cologne lingering behind.

"Good night Mr. Derou," one of his attractive female employees said.

Andre couldn't put a name to her face. He smiled and said, "Good night." She couldn't help but turn around to give him one last glance as he walked away. *Fine ass*, she said to herself.

At Global Consulting, the men aspired to be Andre and well, half the women desired him so badly they would be on their backs in a heartbeat if Andre ever propositioned them. Unfortunately for them, he never crossed that line. He kept it strictly professional at his workplace.

Andre got into his Lamborghini, dropped the top and sped down Broadway Street. Once on the interstate he pressed the gas petal even harder. "Please observe the speed limit," the drivers assist system warned him. He continued to fly up the expressway doing at least ninety miles per hour, until he reached his exit. He then arrived at a gated condominium community. Andre punched in the code and the gate slowly opened. He proceeded through the gate and pulled up to a driveway. He reached the door, turned the key and opened it.

"Baby!" Andre called out. He entered the condo and placed his keys on the kitchen counter. He removed his suit jacket, then threw it over the back of a dining chair. "Baby!" he called out again, walking into the living room. Suddenly he heard footsteps on the stairs.

"What are you doing here?"

"What the hell do you mean?" he asked, frowning.

"Just like I said, what are you doing here? I told you I'm done with you."

"Angelina, you'll never be done with me, not even if you wanted to be," Andre said.

"I'm so sick of your shit!" she spat. "You've been ignoring my calls. Then you take your little bitch on a vacation, come home and I still don't hear from you!"

"Because of that shit you pulled at the charity event. That's why you haven't heard from me."

"So, I'm supposed to just remain a secret right? Our daughter too?"

"I'm not sticking around for this shit!" he said, sharply. Andre turned away and walked towards the kitchen.

"It's not fair to me or Andrea. You said you were going to leave her," she sobbed.

"I've told you already. How many times do I have to tell you. It's not that easy. You're acting as though you didn't know the deal when you met me."

"You're an asshole Andre! You don't care about me!" she said, crying hysterically.

"Who bought you this fancy condo? Or that Porsche parked in the driveway, all that designer shit you got upstairs in the closet? Me!" he said, now raising his voice. "I make sure you and Andrea don't want for shit! So think again before you say I don't care about you!"

"I don't care about any of this materialistic shit," she shot back.

"Yeah, sure you don't," he chuckled, sarcastically.

"All I want is for us to be a family," she said.

"I know what you want," he said, pulling her close to him. He gripped her ass and leaned in for a kiss but she turned away.

"Stop it Andre."

"You sure you want me to stop?" he said, cupping her firm breast and licking her neck.

"Yes. I'm so sick of you," she said, under her breath.

Andre opened her robe, and slid his hands down her panties. He rubbed on her clit, until she could no longer fight it. Her mouth opened and she let out a soft moan.

"I thought you wanted me to stop," he said, teasing her wet pussy. She gave in completely, anxiously undoing his belt and unbuttoning his pants. Andre bent her over the kitchen counter, slapped her on the ass and entered her. He grabbed a fistful of her long natural, curly hair and thrusted his dick in and out of her aggressively. He slapped her on the ass again. "This is all you wanted right!" he said, pumping harder.

"Yes!" she shouted in ecstasy. She repeated, "I love you," over and over again, feeling pain and pleasure at the same time. He felt so good inside of her, but yet, her heart felt heavy because she knew like every other night she would hear the words, "I can't stay."

"I love you Angelina," he said, before climaxing. He exhaled deeply, then pulled up his boxer briefs and pants. She picked up her silk robe from the floor and put it back on.

"You hungry?" she said, wrapping the robe around herself.

"I can't stay baby. I have a few things to take care of."

"You can't stay because you have to get home to your precious wife."

"Here you go again," he said, annoyed.

"Are things ever going to change Andre? I'm tired of being second in your life." Andre just stood there with a blank expression, knowing it was time to go. "I don't understand why it's so hard to leave. You don't have any children with her," she said bitterly.

"I'm not doing this with you Angelina. I can't come here without you constantly hitting me over the head with this dumb shit," Andre said, grabbing his car keys off the kitchen counter.

"Are you going to at least see the baby before you leave?"

"Good night Angelina."

She grabbed him by the arm. "You're not leaving Andre." He yanked away from her, and turned to walk away.

"I hate you!" she shouted, as he walked out the door.

Angelina and Andre were having an affair for over two years. In the beginning, there was never any pressure. She knew her position and she played it well. The fact that he was a married man, didn't faze her one bit. She believed if she played her cards right Andre would eventually leave Maryana and marry her. "Be patient," he would always tell her. "When the time is right, I'm leaving." After two years of hearing the same tired line, she became fed up and was now ready to expose the truth.

A few days later, Andre held a very small but important board meeting to go over the quarterly reports for Global Consulting. He walked into the boardroom at 1:00 p.m. sharp and took the seat at the head of the conference table. Andre's Vice President of Operations, Stanley Kubrick, Senior Marketing Manager, Richard Kern, and Chief Financial Officer, Morris Kent were all present for the meeting.

"Good afternoon everyone."

"Good afternoon sir," they all said in unison.

"Has everyone gotten a copy of the agenda?" Andre asked.

They all nod their head and say, "Yes sir."

"Good. Okay, first I want to start by discussing item one, which is the cost breakdown for the new location. Morris, thank you for emailing the current figures to all of us. I hope that we've all had time to look things over. Morris, is there anything you would like to add before I open this up for questions?"

"No, sir. Nothing has been updated since I last sent the email."

"Are there any questions concerning the report Morris prepared?"

Stanley immediately chimes in. " I'm a bit concerned that IT will have the highest cost attached to this location in terms of moving equipment, contractors, and it will also require a lot of overtime. However, the figures here don't seem to reflect that."

"That is correct," Morris said. "IT is responsible for a large part of the cost, which is why I've allocated some of the cost to the budgets of other departments."

"So does that mean that any IT cost will be covered by the marketing budget?"

"Yes in a way. As you can see here, I've broken down the IT department into segments."

Andre interrupts Morris and Stanley. "Why don't we get back to this later. I don't want to spend too much time on this, since we have a lot to cover. I would like to discuss the earnings, as well as the loss reports."

The intercom buzzed, and Andre's secretary came through the speaker of the telephone. "Mr. Derou, we have an emergency here sir."

"What type of emergency?"

"There are some people here to see you sir, regarding your brother Jackson," she said in a fragile voice.

Jackson was Andre's little brother, a college basketball star, surely on his way to the NBA. Andre tried to stay on him and keep him focused on the right things, but somehow trouble always managed to find him.

"I'll be right there." Andre stood up from the table and said, "Excuse me for a moment. Stanley, will you take over for me?"

"Of course," Stanley replied.

Andre opened the double glass doors and walked out of the boardroom. He walked down the corridor to the reception area to find the security guard having words with a bunch of loud talking people that he didn't recognize. "What's going on here?" Andre said, in a dominant voice.

"What's going on is your little punk ass brother done knocked up my granddaughter and now he's telling her he want nothing to do with her," the older woman said, in a confrontational tone. She looked as though she had just rolled out of bed, wearing an oversized t-shirt, sweats and a scarf wrapped around her head.

"Wait, hold on a minute. This is not the time or place for this. I'm in the middle of handling business. I don't have time for this, nor do I have any control over what Jackson does. I'm not his father."

"I got this grandma," the young and reckless brother said. "Look dog. I don't give a damn about what you talkin' bout right now. Your lil' brother disrespected my lil' sis and I need to holla at him." He was amped up and ready for whatever.

"Should I call the cops sir?" the security guard asked.

"No need for that. Give me a minute," Andre said.

"I just got out of jail and I ain't afraid to go back," he said, pounding his fist into his hands. "I don't give a fuck who you call. We gon' sit down and figure this shit out today. My sister ain't gon be treated like she some hoe."

"Look, I told you once already this is not the time okay," Andre said, highly frustrated but still trying to remain calm. "Now, we can figure this out at another time, but right now I have business to tend to. I need for all of you to leave."

"Look nigga, we ain't going nowhere," he said, getting in Andre's face."

His sister stepped in, and yanked on her brother's arm. "Alright, that's enough Derek. This isn't going to solve anything. Come on, let's go."

Andre noticed her huge belly poking out under her long maxi dress. He could've had them all thrown out in a matter of seconds, instead he tried to come to some sort of resolution, even if it was just temporary.

"What's your name?" he turned to her and asked.

"Ava," she said, in a soft voice.

Andre pulled her to the side and said, "You seem to be the only one with any common sense."

"I apologize for all of this, it's just that Jackson has been taking me through so much. He's telling me I better get an abortion." Her voice and eyes are both sad. "Look at me, do I look like I can get an abortion now?"

"I understand that Ava, but there's nothing we can do about any of that here."

"You're right. Andre I have nothing but the utmost respect for you, and your family, and I just never thought Jackson would do this to me. He knows this is his baby. We were together every day for about ten months. When I first told him I was pregnant he was fine with it, and then all of a sudden he just dropped me."

"Ava, I'll talk to him okay. That's my word. And I'll make sure that he calls you."

"Yeah, you do that!" her brother interjected.

"Thank you, I really appreciate that," Ava said.

Andre sighed deeply and shook his head, as they all walked towards the elevator to leave. "That damn Jackson," he said out loud to himself. He couldn't wait until he saw him face to face, so he could set him straight. Andre went back to the boardroom and closed the meeting. He then went back to his office and sat down at his desk thinking about the craziness that had just taken place. If there was one thing that Andre didn't like; it was chaos. He liked everything around him at his own pace, smooth and easy going, but with Jackson's drama and all of his drama with Angelina, he was definitely feeling uneasy.

As soon as Andre finished up at the office he drove to San Diego State University's campus to meet up with Jackson. Jackson didn't know what his big brother needed to talk to him about but he could tell by the tone of his voice it was something important. As Andre pulled into the campus parking lot in his red Bugatti, all the college kids stared in amazement. He drove around to the back of the gymnasium and parked diagonally in front of the entrance. He got out of the car and walked inside. Jackson was training hard, per usual. Andre sat in the front row of the bleachers and waited for him to finish up his session.

"What's up Dre!" Jackson said, breathing heavy.

"I got a visit today from your friend Ava and her ratchet ass grandmother and brother."

Jackson took a swig of water. "They came to your house?"

"No, they came to my damn office, loud, and disrespectful."

"My bad, bro. I'm bout to call dat bitch right now and check her for dat."

"You don't need to be calling Ava and checking her about a damn thing. You need to be checking yourself."

With a frown on his face he said, "Oh word? It's like that? You don't even know that broad to be rocking out with her like dat."

"Let's get out of here," Andre said, not wanting to embarrass his baby brother in front of his teammates.

Jackson threw his gym bag over his shoulder, and he and Andre walked outside.

"Let me ask you something. Is the kid yours?"

"Man, I don't know."

"What do you mean you don't know?"

"Like I said, I don't know. It could be, could be not. Hell, I won't know till the baby get here and I take a test."

Andre shook his head. "Do you hear yourself? You sound real stupid right now. It could be yours!" he said, mocking him. "You shouldn't even be in this situation again! You didn't learn from the last mistake? Luckily, the last girl had plans for her future and decided not to keep the baby, otherwise you'd be on your second kid. You ain't even made it to the NBA yet, and you can't control yourself."

Jackson leaned up against Andre's car, folded his arms and blew air out of his mouth. Although he was silent Andre could sense his aggravation.

"Look at you. You hate to hear the truth. When are you gonna get it? You have everything going for you right now. But the way you moving is not smart. You need to get your shit together Jackson."

"Like you?" he said sarcastically. "I need to get my shit together like you?"

"This ain't about me. It's about you and your inability to make good choices."

"Man I'm sick and tired of you coming down on me like your shit don't stink. Unlike you Mr. perfect, I don't wear a mask. With me, what you see is what you get. You just running around here pretending to be something that you not!" Jackson said, with anger riding his voice. "If my shit is not right, it's because I learn from you and dad."

"You know what your problem is Jackson? You're so quick to blame everyone else for your fuckups. All I've ever tried to do was look out for you and keep you on the right track."

"Stop talkin' to me like that. I don't need your help. You ain't in no position to talk to me about not fucking up and staying on the right track."

Andre threw his hands up in the air, done with the conversation and ready to walk away, but Jackson was far from finished. "You take a look in the mirror lately? You getting crazy money, big ass house, a dozen cars, and a beautiful wife, but that's not enough is it? You still out here chasing. And you want to talk to me about making bad choices? Yeah, okay," Jackson said walking off. "Get your own shit together first. Then you come talk to me! You hypocrite!"

Andre quickly jumped into his car, and sped out of the parking lot. He had never got into a screaming match with his baby brother before, and it was unsettling for him. Andre was always lecturing him about how to be a man and what not to do. Although he meant well, how could he give any advice on doing what's right, when he didn't walk a straight line himself. He was furious that Jackson had talked to him the way he did. Maybe he was even more furious because he knew that everything Jackson had said was true. To everyone on the outside Andre appeared to have it all together. Some might say he was perfect and that he had the perfect life. Those that truly knew him, the way Jackson knew him would say he learned to cover his dirt to perfection.

CHAPTER FIVE

It was a day like any other day. I got up around 6:00 a.m. and worked out like I did every morning. I showered, then got in the kitchen and whipped up my husband's favorite breakfast. French toast, home fries, cheese eggs and turkey bacon. I carried the breakfast tray upstairs and into our bedroom. Andre was awake but still lying in bed.

"Good morning."

He smiled. "Good morning beautiful."

I put the glass of orange juice on the night stand and placed the tray on his lap. "Breakfast in bed for my King."

"Thank you my Queen."

He immediately dug in, piling his fork with eggs and taking big bites of the French toast, "Mmm, this is good baby."

"Thank you," I said, smiling on the outside as well as the inside. Andre always did like my cooking. That's one of the things I prided myself on, as far as being a housewife. The other was, being able to break him down in the bedroom. He told me I was the first woman to ever match his huge sexual appetite.

"What has you in such a good mood this morning?" he asked.

"I'm in a good mood every morning," I said.

He laughed. "Sure you are honey." Andre knew me too well. He could tell I was up to something.

"When you were away in New York, I reached out to Michael over at Channel 5 news." My voice is soft and hesitant.

"Yeah…" he said, devouring his food.

"They're going to give me a shot!" I exclaimed.

He took a sip of his orange juice. "A shot at what?" he asked, in a dry voice.

"Broadcasting! And no more of that field reporting stuff! They're talking about putting me behind a desk baby!"

"Mary, you're all over the place. First, you want to adopt a baby and now, you want to get a job."

"It's not a job, it's a career and this is something I've always wanted to do."

"I thought being a mother is what you've always wanted."

"Stop saying it as though I have to choose one or the other. Besides, we haven't discussed the adoption since when?" He didn't say anything.

"My point exactly. Andre tell me what you would rather me do? Just sit around and do nothing?"

"Your life is so awful," he said, sarcastically.

"That's not what I'm saying."

"Well then, stop being so dramatic." He got out of bed and headed for the bathroom. I followed behind him. "Mary you've got it made. Most women would die to be in your shoes."

"I don't care about most women. This is about me and what I want." Andre turned the shower on right in the middle of me pleading my case. "But you know what, just forget it," I said, before storming out.

I was upset but mostly with myself. I don't know why I needed his approval so badly. It's not like he ever needed mines. I should've been more selfish, I just didn't know how.

I was headed to the spa. I planned on spending the entire day to myself. I didn't feel like talking to anyone. I didn't want to be bothered at all. It was just one of those days. The way Andre dismissed me earlier didn't sit well with me. He was always gone. Always doing his own thing, and I never complained. Why couldn't he support me the way I supported him for the last seven years? And why didn't he like me at the office? Why did he want me stuck at home? I heard Bree's voice in my head, *Girl, you don't know what he's doing when he's away. You need to do you, because he's damn sure doing him.* Just as I was pulling up to the spa, my cell phone starts ringing. It was Bree. I didn't answer. "Dammit! It's never any fucking parking around here!" I said, in frustration. My cellphone rang again. I see "Bree is calling" flashing across my navigation screen. *What the hell does she want?*

"Hello."

"Mary, where are you? I really need you?"

"I'm just getting to the spa. What's wrong?"

"It's too much to talk about over the phone. Can you please just come over?" she said frantically.

"Yeah, I'll be right there."

"Are you leaving now?"

"Yes Bree, I'm on my way."

There goes my day to myself, I thought to myself. I made a sharp U-turn and headed back in the other direction. It was usually a twenty minute drive to Bree's house from downtown but the way I was driving, I got to her in under fifteen. I texted her when I was five minutes away, so when I pulled up she was outside waiting for me. My Valentino heels click-clacked against the pavement, as I scurried up the stairs.

As soon as we got inside, Bree immediately poured us a drink. "So what's going on?" I asked.

"You're not going to believe this!"

"What?"

"Remember I told you I was going out with Jeff last night?" I nodded yes. "Afterwards, I went back to his place."

"Mmm-hmm."

"You know he's the first guy I actually liked in a really long time."

"Right," I replied.

"Well anyways, I decided to go snooping through his phone. And bitch! I'm beyond disgusted!"

"Oh Lord, I'm afraid to ask...what did you see?"

"Selfies of him and a guy, standing in front of a mirror naked. Jeff was holding the phone and the guy had his hand wrapped around Jeff's dick."

My mouth fell wide open. "You're lying!"

"I'm not even done! Are you ready for this one?"

"Bitch what?" I said in a very dramatic voice.

"I saw a video clip of the guy holding the phone, while Jeff is on top of him sucking his neck and pounding him from behind."

"Okay, I've heard enough. I'm done."

"Crazy right?"

"Beyond crazy."

Bree shook her head in disgust. "Then it all started making sense. Always wanting to fuck me in the ass."

"Straight guys like that too."

"No girl, every time we fucked, he would literally beg me for it."

"Did you ever let him do it?"

"Hellll no! He even had the nerve to ask me to lick his ass."

"Now, that's going too damn far. You didn't see that as a red flag?"

"I didn't think anything of it. I just figured he was a freak."

"My thing is, if you're gay, be gay. Just don't be in the closet," I said, raising my glass of wine to my lips. "I can't stand that down low shit."

"Exactly!" Bree cosigned.

"Hell, with all those damn skeletons he got in his closet, he need a lock on his phone."

She gave me a devilish grin and said, "It was locked. I saw him enter his passcode once before and I remembered it."

"Oh shit," I said, laughing. "So what did you say to him?"

"Nothing right away. I was afraid he would be so ashamed that he would snap and try to hurt me."

"Well I know you started talking shit once you got home."

"You know I did! I went in on that nasty, down low muthafucka!"

"Please tell me you used protection with him."

"Every time," she said. "I don't play around."

"Whew, thank God!" I said, relieved that she was smart enough to protect herself. I was surprised Bree kept Jeff around as long as she did. Most guys didn't last a week. She would always say jokingly, "I don't catch feelings, I catch flights." But I guess there was just something about Jeff, because for the first time in a long time, she caught feelings. I have to say though, after being around him a couple times he even convinced me he was perfect for her. I always thought my gay radar was on point, but Jeff hid it well. I never would've thought he played for both teams.

I spent the entire day at Bree's house. Hours passed and we were still sitting in the same spot on her sofa, drinking and having girl talk. I purposely stayed out late. I wanted Andre to beat me home for a change. You know, wonder where I was or maybe call to see when I was coming home. But it got later and later and Andre never called.

"Andre hasn't called me all day," I said. "As a matter fact, he never calls."

"What do you mean?"

"When we're away from each other, he doesn't call to check on me or anything. It's like, if I don't call, then I won't hear from him." I grabbed the bottle of wine, raised it to my lips and finished it. You would've thought I was drinking truth serum, the way my emotions spewed out. "Sometimes I feel like we live two separate lives." Bree didn't interrupt. She just listened. "It's like he's over there living his life and I'm over here."

"I understand," Bree said.

"Don't get me wrong. I have everything I want and need, materialistically. But I'm lonely. Married but lonely. How is that even possible? I miss those days when we were best friends."

"Let me ask you this...would you rather him be a good friend? Or a good provider?"

"Both."

"Not going to happen. Perfect men, just don't exist," she laughed.

"I'm not asking for perfect. Hell, I'm not perfect. None of us are. I just want to be happy."

Bree paused, looked me in the eye and asked the million dollar question. "Aren't you happy?"

I shrugged my shoulders. "Sometimes…I guess," I said, staring sadly into Bree's eyes.

"Okay, enough of all this soap opera shit. I have just what you need."

Bree went upstairs to her bedroom and came back down with a small box, holding her stash of marijuana. She sat next to me smiling, as she packed the marijuana into the bowl of the pipe. She handed me the pipe and lighter, "Time to cheer up."

I put the pipe between my lips and flicked the lighter. I took a big drag and slowly exhaled it.

"What problems?" Bree said, jokingly.

I just laughed and took another drag off of the pipe. I held it, then exhaled and handed the pipe to Bree. It was exactly what I needed. It allowed me to escape my own mind. I didn't want to think about anything. It was a temporary escape from my reality.

It was close to midnight when I finally got home that night. I took a long hot shower, even shampooed my hair and Andre still hadn't come home yet. I stood in front of my vanity mirror with a towel wrapped around me. I towel dried my hair and then wrapped it in a bun with a scrunchie. I walked over to the dresser and pulled out a pair of red lace cheeky panties and a matching camisole. I dressed, then climbed into bed and reached for the TV remote. I didn't intend on actually watching television. I was beat. Still, I searched for the perfect movie to fall asleep on.

Lifetime it is, I said to myself. I turned on my side, pulled the covers up around my neck and closed my eyes. Before I could fall asleep my cellphone started ringing. I rolled my eyes and sucked my teeth when I saw "unknown caller" flashing across the screen of my iPhone.

"Hello," I answered, with an attitude.

"Is this Maryana?" the voice on the other end asked.

"Who is this?"

"Is this Maryana?" she repeated.

"Look, you called me, didn't you? You know who I am. What do you want?"

"I called to tell you about your husband."

"Who is this? I don't even know who the hell you are."

"My name is Angelina. Listen, I'm not calling you to start any drama or anything like that. I just think you deserve to know the truth."

"There's nothing you can tell me about my husband. I'm hanging up."

"Maryana wait," she said, desperately. "I know that he's not home right now. And I know that because he just left my house."

My heart dropped to my stomach like a rock. I sat up quickly, trying to wrap my mind around what she'd just said. Lost for words, I just held the phone.

"I've been sleeping with your husband for the past two years. We have a six month old daughter. Her name's Andrea."

"Wait, what did you say?"

"We have a daughter. She's six months old."

"I don't believe you. You're lying."

"I don't have any reason to lie to you. Your husband on the other hand, he's the one that's been lying to you."

"Oh, please. You've been supposedly fucking my husband for two years and now all of a sudden you think I deserve to know the truth?" *This bitch has some nerve*, I thought to myself. "I don't have time for this shit."

I hung up the phone. "We have a daughter," kept looping over and over in my head, as I paced the bedroom floor. I knew there had to be some truth to what she'd said. I believed she was sleeping with my husband, but for two years? A baby? No fucking way.

I could hear Andre's car pulling in and the garage door closing. I grabbed my cellphone off the nightstand and flew downstairs to confront him. I anxiously stood at the bottom of the staircase with my arms folded, waiting for Andre to walk through the door.

"Hey Baby."

"Don't hey baby me!" I spat. "I just got off the phone with your bitch! Angelina!"

Andre stood there confused, as if he didn't know what I was talking about.

"Who the hell is Angelina?"

"You tell me! You just left her house didn't you?" I knocked the briefcase out of his hand. You finished work hours ago! Why in the hell are you just now walking through the door?"

"You need to calm down alright. I was out with Devin." He pulled out his cellphone and handed it to me. "Here, you can call him."

"For what? So he can lie for you? Don't play me like I'm stupid Andre."

"Listen to me. I swear to you. I don't know an Angelina. Whoever that was, they're lying to you."

"She said she's been with you for two years and that you have a six month old daughter."

C'mon now, Maryana. Do you hear yourself? That's insane. The bitch is lying! And you're coming at me all crazy, believing everything a stranger has told you about me!" he said, raising his voice.

"Don't try to flip this shit on me Andre."

"I'm not. I'm just saying. All of this is crazy and it makes no sense. Someone is fucking with you. Can't you see that?"

"Why would someone randomly call me and tell me a bunch of lies about you?"

"I don't know. It could be jealousy. Maybe they want what you have."

"Oh yea, I forgot, there's so many women dying to be in my shoes," I said sarcastically. Well, guess what? They can have your sorry ass!"

"Look Maryana. I'm telling you the truth. I'm not cheating on you. I don't know anyone named Angelina and I damn sure don't have a baby." Andre looked me straight in the eye and said, "I would never jeopardize what I have with you for nothing in the world. You understand me?"

I don't know how he did it. No matter how heated an argument got, no matter how upset I was, he was always able to calm me during the storm. Maybe because he was crafty with his words. Always smooth talking me, but no, not this time. I wasn't buying it. We continued arguing that night until he decided he couldn't take anymore. He slept on the other side of the house, in the guest room. For the first time in all the seven years we were together, Andre and I went to bed angry.

The next morning I awoke to the same thoughts which lingered from the night before. I immediately checked my cellphone for any missed calls. I was curious to know if Angelina had called again. She hadn't, but she sent me a text, *It's Angelina. Call me as soon as you can please. It's important.* I went into the bathroom to freshen up. I thought long and hard about whether or not I should call her. If she was telling the truth about everything I knew it would tear me apart. It boiled down to this. Was I going to live happy with Andre's lies or face the sad truth? I went back and forth about it in my head, contemplating what to do. I took a deep breath, picked up my cellphone and dialed Angelina's number.

"Hello."

"What's up? What's so important?"

"Andre called me this morning."

"And?"

"He said he loves me and that he wants us to be a family. As long as I don't contact you again. He wants me to keep my mouth shut. I'm really tired…"

"You're tired of what Angelina? Being his secret? He denied you and your baby! He told me he didn't even know you." Tears welled up in my eyes and my heart started racing. It was clear to me she was telling the truth but I wasn't ready to let her know that. "You're a fucking joke. Don't you see that?"

"I'm a joke? Your husband has been sleeping with me for two years and you didn't even know it! I have his baby! What do you have? A piece of paper? Sounds like the joke is on you," she said spitefully.

"If you have his baby, and that's a big if...I feel sorry for you. If Andre wanted to be with you, why doesn't he just leave me? We don't have any children. It's not that complicated. He doesn't want you. I could leave him today and it still won't be you."

She paused for a few seconds before responding. "Look, I don't want to argue with you." She paused again. "I just want to talk to you woman to woman. That's why I gave you my number. No games, no bullshit. I just want to talk."

"I'm done talking over the phone. Let's meet in person."

"I don't have a problem with that. Where would you like to meet?"

"Could you be at Bayview Park in about an hour?"

"Yea. I can do that."

"Okay, I'll meet you there."

"Maryana, uh, are you coming alone? I don't want any drama."

"Just me. No drama."

"I guess I'll see you then."

"Okay, bye."

"Bye."

I hung up the phone, showered and fixed my hair. I pulled my hair up in a high bun and let my baby hairs fall down over my forehead. I wore a pair of stunning diamond stud earrings that looked perfect with my up-do. I slipped on a cute floral romper and a pair of nude So Kate by Christian Louboutin. I didn't want it to look as though I was trying too hard. I wanted to be semi casual but fly at the same time. I grabbed my Chanel bag, then checked myself out in the mirror before heading out the door.

Andre wasn't home when I left. I didn't plan on telling him where I was going anyways. I didn't want him intervening with his bullshit. It was time for me to find out the truth once and for all. If she did have a baby by my husband I was almost certain she would bring the baby along. She would want me to see her. I was sure of that.

I pulled up to Bayview Park at exactly 1:00 p.m. It was a Saturday, so the park was crowded. Angelina texted me and told me where she'd be sitting. I made my way through the busy park and found her in a quiet spot, sitting on a bench facing the San Diego skyline. As I got closer I could see a baby's stroller next to her and I just wanted to turn and walk in the other direction. Still, I tried to keep my composure as I sat down next to her.

"Hey," she said casually, as if we were friends meeting up for girl talk. Like she wasn't screwing my husband. When Angelina looked up at me my heart sank to my stomach. It was her. The woman from the party.

"It was you. You were at the charity gala."

"Yes, I was."

"What were you doing there?"

"I thought I finally built up enough courage to tell you the truth…but when I saw you, and I saw Andre…I just couldn't."

"Wow," I sighed.

"This is Andrea," she said, lifting the baby gently from the stroller.

In that moment my world came crashing down on me. My entire body went numb. Staring into the baby's pretty little brown eyes, there was no denying she belonged to my husband. She looked exactly like him.

"Does Andre family know about you and the baby?"

"No. I've never met any of his family. He's brought his best friend Devin around but that's about it."

"Devin knows about you?"

"He's the baby's god father."

I shook my head in disgust. "Do you see my husband often?"

"Every day, when we're on good terms."

"Where? Does he come to your house? Or…"

"Mostly. When we first met, we would always go to his house."

My eyes widened. "What do you mean, his house? You've been in our home?" I asked.

"No. He's never taken me to where you guys live. He has another house."

"Another house where?"

"15888 Hardwick Lane," she said.

I couldn't believe what I was hearing. This was Andre's old house. The house he told me he sold years ago, after we got married. I guess he kept it, so he could discreetly do his dirt. I kept replaying Andre's words in my head, *it's all lies. Someone's messing with you. I don't know her.* He looked me right in the eye and lied to my face. We sat out there on the bench and talked for over an hour. Angelina filled me in on the life she shared with my husband. Teary eyed, she confessed her love for him and even told me that he'd been taking very good care of her and the baby. She went on to tell me about all the times she accompanied him on business trips and all the times he lied to me and said he was going away, so that he could spend a few days with her. The more she told me, the more I could feel parts of myself slipping away. I tried to hold it together. I couldn't break down in front of my husband's mistress. How pathetic would that be? I couldn't stand her knowing the truth. She'd gotten the best of me and I felt as though I had lost. A baby? How could I compete with that?

The minute I got into my car, tears poured down my face. The pain I felt was unbearable. My tires screeched as I swung my Ferrari out onto the busy street, without stopping to look out for oncoming traffic. Traffic skidded to a stop and horns beeped at me as I sped off. I kept seeing Andrea's face. I couldn't shake that painful image. My heart felt heavy in my chest. I couldn't breathe. I couldn't think. All I could do was cry. I pressed down on the gas pedal even harder, swerving in and out of traffic, hoping to crash. Not that I wanted to die. I just desperately needed to snap out of this moment…I could feel my sanity slipping fast.

CHAPTER SIX

For me, it was a cold day in July. One I never saw coming. The day I learned the ugly truth. I'd been betrayed by the one person I loved more than anything in the world. How did I not know my husband was having an affair for two years? Were there signs all along and I hadn't been paying attention? I found myself overthinking. So many unanswered questions. It was like a puzzle in my mind and I struggled to put the pieces together.

I knew Andre would deny Angelina and the baby till the end. He would never admit to any of it, not even if I told him I met with her. I would have to confront him with solid proof. I texted Angelina and asked her to send me any pictures she had of them together. She went above and beyond. She sent me screenshots of their text messages and what really put the nail in Andre's coffin were the pictures from the day their baby was born. He was right at her side when she gave birth to the baby and the smile on his face while holding Andrea, spoke volumes.

All eyes were on me as I stomped my way to my husband's office. My heels clicked loudly against the marble floor and my emotions were visible all over my face. It was impossible for me to mask my anger. I could feel it brewing inside of me like a volcano ready to erupt.

I barged into Andre's office, "You lying son of a bitch!"

"Not today Maryana, especially not at my place of business."

I walked up to him, got real close and said, "Fuck you and your business. You lied to my face."

"I didn't lie to you but if you want to take a complete stranger's side over mine, then fine."

"I met with her Andre."

"You met with who?"

"Angelina."

He threw his hands up in the air, as if he'd had enough. "Now you're taking this way too far. Have you lost your mind?"

"I'm only going to ask you this one more time. Do you have a baby with her?"

"No, hell no!" he said, angrily.

"So, you don't know her right?"

"No. I told you that already. I swear on my dead grandmother's grave that I..."

Before he could even get the entire lie out I cut him off. "Oh, don't you fucking dare." I reached into my bag and grabbed my cellphone. I pulled up the pictures Angelina sent me and put my phone in his face. "What is this? Isn't this you?" He glanced at my phone and dropped his head low. "Now what? What's your excuse now?" He just sat there with a pathetic look on his face. "You have a baby

Andre…you have a family." Tears rolled down my face and when I looked at him I didn't see the man I spent the last seven years with, I saw a stranger.

"That's not true. You're my family."

"Then why lie to me Andre? What about the house you told me you sold years ago?"

"What house?"

"You know what I'm talking about Andre. Everything you've told me has been a lie. Our marriage is one big lie."

"I don't know what you want me to say."

"I just want the truth. I need to hear the words come out of your mouth. I already know, but I need you to say it."

He exhaled deeply as he put his head in his hands. He stayed silent for at least a minute and just stared down at the floor.

"You can't hurt me more than you've already hurt me Andre. Just tell me the truth."

He looked up at me with sad eyes and said, "It's true. All of it. I did sleep with her…and uh…the baby…she's mine," he stuttered.

"Andre you did more than sleep with her. You had a relationship with her for two years," I sobbed. I tried to control my tears but I couldn't. I thought I would feel relieved once he finally told me the truth. I was wrong.

He stood up in front of me and attempted to wrap his arms around me. "Come here."

"Don't fucking touch me," I cried. "I don't even know who you are anymore. You destroyed everything we had. I will never look at you the same."

"I'm sorry Maryana. I'm so sorry for hurting you."

"You're not sorry for hurting me. You're only sorry you got caught. And you know what, Angelina has finally gotten what she wanted. She can have you! Go be with her and your baby! I'm done!"

"What do you mean, you're done?"

"You'll see," I said, storming out of his office.

Andre must've left the office right after me because as soon as I got home, he walked in five minutes later. I didn't think he had the guts to come home. I thought he would stay away and at least give me time to cool off. Instead, he made matters worse.

"We can get past this."

"How are we supposed to do that when you laid down and made a baby with someone else? She's only six months! We can't get past this! Do you have any idea how I feel right now? It feels like you ripped my heart out of my chest," I sobbed.

"I know sorry is not going to change things but if you let me, I promise you I will make this right."

"Do you love her?"

"Who?"

"Who else!" I yelled. "Angelina! Your baby mother! Do you love her?"

"I got love for her. I mean, I care about her," he said, not even able to look me in the eye. I just stood there in silence. "In a way, I feel like this baby is a blessing to us," he said in a low voice.

"Who do you mean us?"

"Me and you."

My face twisted in annoyance and before I could even get a word out he says, "Just hear me out. I wanted children with you more than anything and I know you wanted the same but things didn't work out the way we planned. I know I lied and I cheated but look, now we have Andrea."

"So you think the baby you had with your side bitch is a blessing to me? Ahhh!" I screamed, lunging at him, swinging my fist, landing one punch after another. "I hate you!"

He grabbed both of my arms in an effort to restrain me. "Calm down Mary."

"Fuck you!" I spat.

"I think I should leave," he murmured.

"Yeah, that's right. Leave! Get the fuck out!" I said, sharply.

"Let me grab some of my things."

"No, you're going to leave now! Get out!" I shouted from the top of my lungs. "Go to your bitch! Isn't that what you've been doing for the past two years, you piece of shit!"

The door slammed behind him. The moment he walked out the door I felt regret. As hurt as I was and as much as I wanted our marriage to be over, the truth of the matter was that I wasn't ready to lose him to her. Why should she win? Who the hell did she think she was? Don't get me wrong, I blamed Andre for everything. He was the one that betrayed me. He gave her the ammunition to destroy me and our marriage but still, I wasn't going to just step aside and let them be one big happy family.

A few days passed and I hadn't seen Andre. He called and texted a few times, but that was about it. Even though I didn't answer for him or reply to his text messages, I expected for him to try a little harder. He didn't even bother coming home. It seemed as though he'd given up on us and that hurt worse than the affair. I found myself sinking deeper and deeper into depression. I laid in bed all day, every day, torturing myself with thoughts of Andre being with Angelina and their child. It literally made me sick. I couldn't eat nor could I sleep. I didn't want to talk to anyone, not even Bree. I had over one hundred missed calls and text messages. Half of them were from her. I knew it was only a matter of time before she came over.

The first day Bree showed up at my door I didn't let her in. She rang the doorbell several times and called my phone repeatedly. It's not that I didn't want to see her, but I knew I would have to explain everything that happened over the last few days and I just didn't have the energy.

The very next day Bree was back again. It was around 11a.m. when she came banging on my door like she was the police. I went into the bathroom to check myself out, I looked terrible. My eyes were puffy and bloodshot red from crying myself to sleep the night before. I splashed cool water on my face and dabbed it dry with a towel, but that couldn't erase the sadness written all over my face. I grabbed my favorite robe, slipped on my Chanel slippers and took my time going downstairs, hoping she'd just leave. She knocked again. "Girl you better open this door, I'm not leaving!" she shouted. I hesitated for a second and took a deep breath before opening the door.

"Are you okay? I've been calling and texting you." I didn't say anything. I just shook my head no. "I spoke to Andre and he said, ya'll had a fight."

And that's when I broke down in tears. "My heart hurts so bad. He hurt me so bad, I don't know what to do," I cried, hysterically.

Bree wrapped her arms around me and I cried like a baby on her shoulder, "Aww boo, it's going to be okay."

"I don't think so."

We walked into the living room and sat down on the sofa. "Tell me what happened," Bree said.

"You were right. You were right about everything," I said, sniffling.

Bree has a confused look on her face. "About what?"

"Andre. He's been cheating on me." I paused and tried to get a hold of my emotions, but I just couldn't stop the tears from flowing. "He's been cheating on me for two years."

"What! With who?"

"Her name is Angelina. Do you remember I told you about the blocked calls? She nods yes. "It was her. Remember at the charity gala, I told you there was a woman staring at me?" She nods yes again. "That was also her."

Bree shook her head in disbelief. "Wow. I'm lost for words."

"That's not even the worst part."

"It gets worse?"

"They have a six month old daughter together."

"No! I don't believe Andre would be that stupid. Not a baby."

"Well believe it. I saw the baby with my own eyes. She looks exactly like him Bree."

"You actually saw the baby?"

"Yeah, I met up with her over the weekend. She brought the baby with her."

"Of course she did," Bree interrupts.

"Bree when I saw that baby my heart dropped."

"I can only imagine. So, what happened next?"

"We just talked about everything. She's been away with him on his business trips, he's even lied to me about going away, so he could spend nights with her. She told me he bought her a condo, brand new car and takes care of her and the baby very well."

"Damn," Bree says, shaking her head. "So what is Andre saying about everything?"

"When I first confronted him about it he denied everything. He told me he didn't even know her and that someone was just messing with me." I started to cry again. "He looked me right in the eye and lied to my face."

Bree put her arm around me. "Boo, don't cry, you're going to make me cry too."

"Angelina sent me screenshots of text messages he sent her and pictures of them together, so I confronted him again and that's when he finally told me the truth."

"So what is he saying? Is he going to end it with her?"

"I think he loves her Bree."

"Why do you say that?"

"Because I asked him if he was in love with her and he couldn't even say no. He tells me that he has love for her and that he cares for her."

"He doesn't love that bitch. She's just something to do."

"C'mon Bree, for two years? He has to love her. Why keep her around for two years?"

"Because he didn't get caught. Cheating is always fun, until you get caught."

"Yeah I know but this is different. She has his child."

"So what, you're his wife! What are you going to do? Are you just going to walk away and let her have your husband?"

"The question isn't what I'm going to do. It's what he's going to do. If he doesn't care, then why should I?"

"He cares Maryana."

"Well then why isn't he here?" Bree just looked at me and didn't say anything. "I feel like a fucking fool. How did I not know? Hell, even you knew he was cheating."

"You trusted that your husband was being faithful. That doesn't make you a fool."

I broke down and started crying even more. Like I expected, rehashing everything only made me feel worse. I cried so hard, Bree cried too. I told her I didn't want to talk about it anymore and that I just needed to be alone. She said, "we're done talking about it, but I'm not leaving you."

A week had gone by and Andre still hadn't come home. I hadn't heard from Angelina either, which led me to believe she was content. Her mission was accomplished. She finally got what she wanted, and that was my husband. I didn't understand how he could be so nonchalant after hurting me the way he did. Even though in my mind I was done with Andre, I still wanted him to put up a fight. Him staying away, cut deeper and deeper every single day.

Sunlight beamed through my window and onto my face, awaking me. I looked up and saw Bree pulling the curtains back. I gave her a key to the house, since she'd been coming over every day to check on me. She picked up the empty vodka bottle that lay on the floor, then sat it on the nightstand next to another empty bottle of tequila. She then sat next to me on the bed.

"C'mon Mary, you have to get up and pull yourself together."

"I'm fine."

"You're not fine. You've been in bed for a week straight."

"It hasn't been a week." My voice is monotone and dry.

"Girl what are you talking about? It's Tuesday…again." She pulled the covers off me. "Get up, we're getting out of this house today."

"Not today Bree, I don't feel like going anywhere."

"I don't care. I'm not going to just let you sit around and be miserable."

"Who says I'm miserable?"

"Girl, bye. Go look in the mirror. You don't even look like yourself. Have you been eating?" I didn't answer her. I just laid there feeling sorry for myself. "Look, I know you're hurting but don't let him keep you down this way. Do you think he's somewhere curled up in bed, crying his eyes out?"

"No," I murmured.

"Exactly. So, get your pretty ass out of bed, get yourself together and let's be out," she demanded.

I sighed. "Okay, okay."

"I'll be downstairs waiting for you."

I sluggishly got out of bed and walked into the bathroom. I stood there in front of the mirror for at least a minute staring into my own eyes, trying to remember who I was before all of this. How could I be so stupid? Stupid enough to make Andre the center of my universe. I should've known better than to revolve my life around him. Now that Andre was gone, I felt lost, like I had no purpose, or sense of direction. Before all of my husband's dark secrets came to light I thought I was the luckiest woman in the world. Every morning I woke up to this lavish life, lying next to the man I nearly worshiped, you couldn't tell me I didn't have it made. But now, even with all the money, a big beautiful mansion, designer clothes, exotic cars parked in the garage, my world felt smaller than ever.

While showering I decided I was going to visit Andre's mother, Eve. Over the years I grew extremely close to both of his parents, but his mom and I had a special kind of bond. I admired and respected her a great deal. She married Andre's father at a young age, raised three boys, maintained her home life, and professional career. She always said I was the daughter she never had, and to me, she was the mother I always wished I had. I couldn't wait to see Eve, so I could tell her about everything that transpired.

Andre's father, Kenneth greeted Bree and I at the door with a smile and a big hug. "You just missed your husband," he said, as he closed the door behind us.

"Oh, really?" I said, trying to hide my annoyance.

"Yup, just ten minutes ago. He'll be back, he went with Jackson to meet with his new agent."

"Oh okay," I said. "Where's mom?"

"She's out back."

"Where's that fine ass son of yours," Bree mumbled, referring to Andre's oldest brother Adrian.

I giggled at her. "Shut up crazy."

Bree stayed inside, while I went outside to chat with Eve. I walked out back and there she was, sitting on a swinging bench that overlooked her beautiful garden. Her face immediately lit up as soon as she saw me. I wrapped my arms around her, and she squeezed me tight, then kissed me on the cheek.

"Mom I really need to talk to you."

"I can already see that just by looking in your eyes. What's wrong baby?"

I sat down next to her. "Andre's having an affair."

She looked shocked and disappointed at the same time. "Oh honey, I'm sorry."

"It's been going on for two years and he has a baby with her."

"A what!? He has a what!?" she says, in a stern motherly voice.

"Yes mom. I've seen the baby and I'm sad to say it but it's true." My eyes immediately start to water. "Mom I don't know what to do. I feel so lost in all of this. Andre left, I haven't seen him in a week. He's not even trying to make this right. I'm just left to pick up the pieces and I don't know where to begin. I'm hurting so bad," I cried.

"Come here sweetie." She cradled me in her arms like a baby, rubbing my back, while repeatedly telling me not to cry.

"It just hurts so bad," I sobbed.

"I know it does, but you know what, it's not going to hurt for long. You know why?"

I look up at her with sad eyes. "Why?"

"Because as of today, you're done waiting on Andre to fix it. God is going to fix it. He's going to mend that broken heart, you hear me? I nod yes. "As long as you look to a man to mend you when you feel you've been broken, you'll end up disappointed every time."

"You're absolutely right."

"Everything is going to be okay. Trust that."

"Mom can I ask you a personal question?"

"Of course you can."

"Has Andre's father ever cheated on you?"

"As a matter of fact, he has. He's cheated on me more than once," she said, staring me straight in the eye. "We've been married thirty-eight years and it hasn't been easy. Things weren't always peaches and cream. Lord knows we've had our share of ups and downs, but we got through them."

"How did you get through it?"

"Forgiveness. Without it, I don't think we'd be together today."

"Did you ever feel like walking away?"

"Not once," she said without hesitation. "My husband has made some terrible decisions but even so, his bad never outweighed his good."

"I have to be honest with you, I don't want to walk away from Andre. I still love him and want to make it work but I'm just not sure I can. I can get past the affair, but I don't think I can get past this whole baby thing."

"I think you can, eventually. Right now it's too soon to even consider. You need time to heal."

"You're right mom."

"What is that fool saying about everything?"

"That's the thing, he's not saying anything. I haven't heard from him. I don't know, maybe he's staying away because I was so angry, I hit him and I…"

"Don't start blaming yourself. He's staying away because he's being a coward. He can't face you like a man," she interrupted.

"You're right."

"And how old is this baby?"

"Six months."

Eve shook her head and said, "Hmp hmp hmp. That's a damn shame."

"Mom do you think he loves her?" I said, as if she was some sort of psychic or something.

"I don't know baby but trust me I'm going to get to the bottom of this. We're going to have a long talk when he gets back."

"Okay mom, I don't want to be here when he gets back."

"I understand but listen, no more worrying, hear me? You're too beautiful, too intelligent and you're too much of a good person. He's my son and I love him dearly but I'm a woman first. You have way too much going for yourself to tolerate any of his bullshit." I slowly nodded in agreement. "As much as I want to see you two work this out, if you can't, know that I'm on your side. I love you and I'm here for you no matter what."

"I know, and I love you too," I said, as she wrapped her arms around me and hugged me.

I walked away from Eve that day feeling much lighter. However, once I got in the car my mind drifted off. I thought about everything that happened. I thought about my marriage and if I could get past what he'd done. I didn't know. I was still confused about that part. What I did know was that I was done crying, done feeling sorry for myself. More importantly, I was done waiting for Andre to fix things. Did I still love my husband? Yes. Did I want to work it out? Yes. At the same time, I realized that if it truly was the end and our marriage was broken, then I was prepared to leave the pieces right where they lay and move the hell on. Well, at least that's what I thought.

CHAPTER SEVEN

The next morning, I packed my suitcase and booked a first class flight out of California. I never thought I'd see the day where I would be back where it all started, the one place I was so desperate to escape. After six years of staying away I found myself back home in Queens, New York. After Ashton died I told myself I would never go back. Everything about home reminded me of her. It forced me to remember how she left me, and then that only made me think that maybe things would've been different if my mother was a better parent. If she loved us the way a mother is supposed to love her children, then maybe Ashton would still be alive and maybe I wouldn't have given my entire life to the first man that said, "I love you."

My flight got in late Wednesday night around 11 o'clock. Good thing I made arrangements for car service. My driver was outside waiting for me at baggage claim pickup. He took my luggage from me and then opened the back door for me to get in. He put my luggage in the truck, then hurried back to the driver's seat.

"Where to ma'am?"

"The Four Seasons on 57th."

Like always, the traffic was bumper to bumper. I didn't arrive at the hotel till an hour later. I tipped my driver a crisp one-hundred dollar bill, and asked if he could be on call for me during my stay.

"Absolutely," he said, smiling from ear to ear, as he tucked the one-hundred dollar bill into his suit-jacket pocket. He reached into his pants pocket and pulled out a business card.

"My cellphone number is there. Call me when you need me and I'll be right here to get you," he said.

"Thank you," I said, returning his smile.

After checking in at the front desk, a bellhop in a navy blue uniform took me upstairs to the 52nd floor and showed me to my lavish penthouse suite. The moment I stepped inside I wished I hadn't. Just being there brought back memories of the night Andre got down on one knee and proposed to me in the middle of Times Square. We stayed at that very same hotel, except we couldn't afford a 50,000 dollar a night suite back then. Still, it was the fanciest room I'd ever stayed in. Walking in together holding hands with him made me feel like Ginger from Casino, when Sam Rothstein upgraded her entire lifestyle.

"Is everything okay?" the bellhop asked,

snapping me out of my daydream.

"Oh, yes, everything's fine," I said. "Before you go, can you turn the air down? It's freezing."

"Will do. Can I do anything else for you?"

"No, thank you," I said, reaching into my handbag. I handed him a fifty-dollar bill.

"My pleasure," he replied. "Thank you. Enjoy the rest of your night Miss."

I opened the sliding glass door and walked out onto the large balcony. As I stared out to the city, I got lost in my thoughts. *As long as we have each other then we have everything we need.* I could hear Andre's voice telling me that. *I can't wait to make you my wife. You'll see, I'm going to spend the rest of my life making you happy.* I had to snap myself out of it. I didn't fly all the way across the country to reminisce about the promises Andre had made. I came home for peace of mind and to find myself again. I needed to let go of all the pain and resentment I held onto for so many years and in order for me to do so, I would have to see my mother.

The next morning I woke up early, showered, dressed, and then ordered room service. Around 1 o'clock I called my driver to pick me up. After my grandmother died my mother moved into her house, which was hard for me to understand because my mother always told my sister and me she hated that house, and that there were too many bad memories. I remember asking, "What happened to you in that house?" And she said, "Too many things that shouldn't have happened." Whenever we went to visit my grandmother, my mother would always be in a rush to leave. I can't remember a single time when we spent more than a couple of hours there, and she never let Ashton and I spend the night.

When I arrived at my grandmother's house I sat in the car for a few minutes before getting out. I was nervous and didn't know how she would feel about me just popping up after six years. I thought, *maybe I should've called first* and then I thought, *she's your mother, you have every right to drop in on her.* After going back and forth about it in my head, I built up enough courage to get out of the car and walk to the front door. My heart was racing, as I rang the doorbell. What a shame I was so nervous to see my own mother but that's just how out of touch we both were. I stood there fidgeting, waiting for someone to open the door, and then suddenly I heard my mother's voice call out, "Who is it?"

I hesitated before answering. "It's me, Maryana."

As my mother turned the lock, I motioned with my hands to the driver that it was okay to leave. "Mary!" she exclaimed behind the door. As soon as the door swung open and she saw my face her eyes opened wide, and a look of excitement appeared on her beautiful face.

"Hey mom," I said, in a semi-awkward voice. The expression on my mother's face went from excitement to confusion rather quickly. "What are you doing here? Is everything okay?"

"I'm okay. I came to see you, that's all."

"Well, aren't you going to give your mother a hug?" she asked, standing in the doorway.

"I'm sorry mom," I said, wrapping my arms around her.

She hugged me back and then said, "Come on. Let's go inside."

We walked in and she closed the door behind us. The house looked completely different than the last time I was there. The walls were freshly painted, the carpet was pulled up, and there was brand new furniture.

"Wow, I see you fixed the house up."

"Yeah, I had to bring some life back into this place."

"It looks nice," I said, nodding my head with a smile.

"You hungry baby?"

"No I'm okay."

"You want something to drink?"

"Yeah, sure," I said, following her into the kitchen.

She opened the refrigerator and pulled out a carton of Lemonade and Cranberry juice. "Lemonade or Cranberry Mary?"

"Lemonade."

She reached into the cabinet, grabbed two glasses and then poured us both a drink.

"I see you kept the table."

"You know how much your grandmother loved this table."

"Yeah, I know," I said, as I rubbed my hands across the shiny cherry wood.

My mother placed the glass of lemonade in front of me, and then sat down next to me. "Now let's cut to the chase Mary. Tell me what's going on," she said, bluntly.

"There's nothing to tell."

"I'm your mother. The second I looked at you I could see that something was wrong. I don't care how long you stay away from me, you're still my daughter."

I sighed, and shook my head, highly annoyed at this point. "After all this time, why can't you just be happy to see me?"

"Oh, so is that it? I should drop down to my knees and praise you for finally coming to see your mother."

I sucked my teeth, and rolled my eyes. "Here we go," I said under my breath.

"I haven't seen you in six years Maryana. Six years!" she said, raising her voice. "I can't call you when I want, I don't know where you live…I'm looking at this big ring on your finger and I don't even know who the hell you're married to!"

"I shouldn't have come here," I said, getting up from the table.

"There you go running again. When are you

going to learn Maryana? You can't keep running away from your problems."

I turned my head sharply towards her. "And you're the one to talk? You think you're so perfect that you can give me advice? You never were a mother to me. And you damn sure weren't a mother to Ashton. You gave up on her. You let her die!"

"That's a terrible thing to say."

"It's the truth and you know it."

"Who taught you to be so cold Maryana?"

"You did," I said, looking her in the eye."

"I wasn't the best mother to you and Ashton, I know that. But I wanted to be. And I tried." My mother's voice began to crack and I could see the tears building up in her eyes. "You don't know what it was like for me okay."

"I know you hated being a mother."

"That's not true. You and Ashton were the only good that came from me. I loved you. Both of you." She took a long pause as the tears streamed down her face. "If I had a hard time showing it, it's because no one ever showed me how to love. When I was little my father showed his love by sneaking into my room at night, and your grandmother, hated me because of it."

"Mom," I said, in a sad voice, placing my hand on top of hers.

"She knew what he was doing to me all those years and she did nothing to stop it. I left home when I was sixteen, and I stayed away for two years. I didn't see my mother till after Ashton was born."

"What about your father?"

"When I left home, that was the last time I saw him. When he died, I didn't even go to his funeral."

I searched for the right words to say, but nothing came to mind. I was speechless. My mother quickly straightened up her face, dried her eyes and said, "You want to know the reason why I moved into this house?"

"Why?"

"I was tired of hiding. Tired of pretending what happened to me didn't happen. I needed to face my demons."

"What your father did to you happened in this house?"

She nodded yes. "The day I moved in here, I took my power back," she said, proudly. "I'm not telling you all of this because I want you to feel sorry for me. I just want you to understand me."

Although I had a better understanding of who my mother was, I couldn't help but feel sorry for her. Growing up, I was ashamed of everything. I was ashamed of where I lived, ashamed of the man my mother chose as my father, and most importantly I was ashamed of her.

"I was only eighteen when I gave birth to your sister, her daddy up and left me when I was three months pregnant. Then I had you at twenty, and I was in love with your father. I thought I was going to spend the rest of my life with him."

Ugh! I hated when she talked about my father in that way. It made me sick to my stomach. "Why did you think that? How could you possibly think you were going to spend the rest of your life with a married man?"

My mother smiled and shook her head as though she was remembering good times. She told me she was in a really dark place when she'd met my father, but he pulled her out of that. He made her smile again, and feel loved. "He was the first man to ever make me feel that way," she said.

My father never denied his wife to my mother. In fact, he told her that he loved his wife very much, but that he was in love with her too. He told my mother, "I'm not leaving her for you, and I'm not leaving you for her." But my mother would have to abide by all of his rules, and when she didn't agree to have an abortion, he left her and never came back.

"I just thought that eventually he would come around, especially once he saw you. You looked so much like him. I didn't think he would ever be able to deny you." She sighed deeply. "But I was wrong."

My mother walked into a post office in Queens one summer with me and Ashton. I was just ten months old. As we were coming in, my father was on his way out. She locked eyes with my father, he took one look at me, and continued walking out the door as if we were strangers. She went after him, holding Ashton's hand and with me in her arms.

"Martino! Martino, wait!" He just kept walking, got into his car and drove off. That was the last time she saw my father. What he did to my mother changed her forever. She never looked at men quite the same again.

"I made a lot of mistakes with you and Ashton, and I know you hate me for that.

"I don't hate you mom."

"You blame me for what happened to your sister."

"I'm sorry for what I said. It's not fair for me to put that on you. I just always felt like she didn't need those doctors or all that medication. All she needed was for us to be there for her."

"And you're right. I wasn't there for her the way I should've been, and I'll regret that for the rest of my life. But please don't punish me for the mistakes I've made. You staying away from me for as long as you did hurt me to my heart. You're my daughter, and I love you."

"I love you too mom, and I'm sorry I stayed away so long."

"I didn't know when I'd see you again, but I knew you'd come home one day."

We both stood up from the table and embraced in a long hug. "You're all I have left in this world," she said, sincerely.

I stayed and talked with my mother until the sun went down. Forgiving my mother was almost therapeutic. I felt as though a weight had been lifted off my shoulders, and now I could finally let go of the past. But still, there was one more thing I needed to address before I left home.

The next day my mother and I went to visit Ashton's grave. It was one of the hardest things I've ever had to do. For years, I dreaded this day. I tried to ignore it. I tried to forget about it. Although I loved Ashton deeply, and missed her very much, I didn't want to acknowledge what happened. I never talked about her to anyone, and I never, not once, visited her gravesite. It was the only way I knew how to cope.

I kneeled down at my sister's grave with tears rolling down my cheeks. I placed my hand flat on the headstone and rubbed my fingers over the inscription that read, "That whosoever believeth in him, should not perish, but have eternal life."-John 3:15

"Hey Ash, it's me. I hope you're not mad at me. I know I should've come to see you sooner," I said, sniffling. "It was just hard for me to accept that you're no longer here. I wish I could've been there to talk to you that day. I didn't know you were in so much pain. I'm sorry, I didn't know. I miss you so much. I wish you were here. So many days, I needed your advice. Every day I wish I could pick up the phone and hear your voice. You were my best friend. And you still are. I know you're looking out for me, like you always have. I love you Ash, always and forever."

My mother and I stayed at Ashton's gravesite for

a while. I think together we bonded in a way we never had before. We placed a bouquet of flowers on Ashton's grave, and said our goodbyes. My mother took my hand, and as we were walking back to the car she turned to me and said, "I know you might not want to hear this, but I'm going to say it anyway. When you showed up at my door I could see that you're in pain. You don't have to say anything. I'm your mother. I can feel it when you're not okay. I just want you to know I never had to worry about you. You were always a fighter Maryana. You're strong. Stronger than you know." She raised her hand to my face, and caressed my right cheek. "The thing about running sweetheart is when you stop, your problems don't. Take it from me, you've got to face them head on."

CHAPTER EIGHT

"**Y**ou look like you struggling over there with that thirty pounder," Andre said, to Devin, laughing. "My wife is in better shape than you."

"Ahh man, whatever," he chuckled, as he continued doing arm lifts with the weights. "Speaking of wifey, what's been going on with ya'll two?"

Sitting up on the weight bench Andre dropped his head in his hands. "I don't know man. I can't even tell you."

"You don't know?" he asked with a confused look on his face.

"I haven't seen her in over a week. I called her a few times but she didn't answer for me. I went by the house a few times but she hasn't been there. I don't know, maybe she's been staying at Bree's."

Devin shook his head. "Damn bro."

"Man, this whole thing with Angelina just blew up in my face."

"I hate to say I told you so, but, I told you so," Devin said, finishing his last rep of arm lifts. "You took things way too far with that girl. Having an affair is one thing. Keeping it going for two years and having a baby is another."

"I know I fucked up," Andre admitted. "And I don't know how I'm going to fix it. I didn't see any of this coming. I never thought Angelina would play me out like that." Andre laid back down on the bench, grabbed the heavy weight bar and continued doing presses.

"It wasn't about playing you. It was about playing Maryana. She put you out there, thinking wifey would pack up and leave."

Andre slowly pushed the weight bar to a locked arm position, exhaled deeply, and then placed the bar back in the holder over his head. After finishing his last set, he grabbed his towel and wiped the sweat off his forehead. "I know you're right but damn! After everything I've done for her. When I met Angelina she was a broke, twenty-three old art student, driving a beat up 1992 Honda Civic. I took her from rags to riches. I give her whatever she ask for. I make sure her and the baby are good. I mean damn, what more does she want?"

Devin chuckled. "Like I said, she wants your wife out of the picture."

"Well, that's not going to happen. I'm not leaving Maryana for her or anybody else."

"So, I guess you're going to leave Angelina then huh?"

"I didn't say that either."

"Game over. It's impossible to play both sides now and after everything that's happened, why would you even want to?"

"I'm not leaving Angelina either."

"Somebody has to be let go Dre."

"And this is coming from the man whose never been faithful to any woman a day in his life."

Devin smirks a little. "And I've never been married a day in my life," he says. "Look man, I'm not judging you. All I'm saying is, man up and make a decision. If you want to make it work with your wife then let Angelina go."

"It's not that easy."

"Why isn't it?"

"She has my baby girl."

"And you're her father. Leaving Angelina won't change that."

"If I break things off with her, she'll take my daughter away from me."

Devin shook his head. "She has you right where she wants you."

"And where's that?"

"By the balls."

They both laughed. "C'mon let's hit the treadmill," Andre says.

"Hey man, I have to ask. Out of all the women, all the women you've cheated on Maryana with, why Angelina?"

"What do you mean?" Andre said loudly, over the sound of his feet pounding against the treadmill.

"You never kept any of the others around. Why her? How'd you get caught up?"

"I never meant for things to go this far with Angelina. We were just having fun. She wasn't looking for anything serious, and she respected my situation. Everything was cool."

"Until she caught feelings," says Devin.

"Exactly…and the rest is history bro."

If anyone knew all the dirt Andre had done over the years, it was his right hand, Devin. They were best friends since high school. Growing up, Andre and his brothers always went to private schools. Andre hated it. He wanted to experience what it was like going to public school. Although his mother was against it, his father allowed him to go during junior year. That's when he met Devin. It wasn't a bad school academically but socially it was a lot different from what Andre was used to. On his first day, a couple of kids tried to scare him into buying them lunch. Andre was standing in the cafeteria line about to pay for his food and two guys walked up on him. One of them said, "Lunch on you." Andre replied, "Naw." Then the other guy said, "we're not asking." Andre didn't back down. Right before a fight broke out between the three of them, Devin stepped in and intervened. No one ever tried him. He was one of the tough guys, sometimes even a bully. From that day forward, Devin and Andre always looked out for one another. Now fourteen years later, they were more like brothers.

"So what's your plan bro?"

"I'm going to fix things with my wife."

"And what about Angelina?"

"I can handle her too. You know uh, I think you underestimating your boy a little bit," Andre said, arrogantly.

"I don't know about all that but what I do know is, you're playing with fire and when you play with fire you get burned."

"You sound like my mother," he said, jokingly. "Trust me, I've got it all under control."

Andre had no intentions on breaking things off with Angelina. His plan was to get things back on track with Maryana, and continue on with Angelina like he'd been doing for the last two years. He did love his wife. He loved her deeply, but he was too selfish to do the right thing. Too selfish to remain faithful. He had the mindset like he was untouchable. Like, he could do anything he wanted and not have to face the consequences of his actions.

Since Andre left home, he'd been staying at his other house, the one he managed to keep a secret from Maryana. This pissed Angelina off because she was certain that she would be waking up to him every morning, now that she exposed the truth. Things weren't exactly going the way she planned but still, she became excited whenever she heard him turn the key in the lock.

"Say hi, daddy!" Angelina said, in her baby voice, waving Andrea's little hand.

Andre walked up and kissed her on both cheeks.

"Hey, pretty girl."

"I don't get a kiss?"

"I just came to check on Andrea. That's it."
Angelina placed the baby in the playpen that lay in the middle of the living room floor. She walked closely to Andre and grabbed the crotch of his pants.

"I know that's not all you came for," she said, biting down on her bottom lip.

Andre backed away from her. "Stop it."

"How many times do I have to say I'm sorry? It's been over a week, and you're still stuck on that shit."

"You shouldn't have done it. You crossed the line Angelina!"

"And I said I was sorry."

"That doesn't change anything. You betrayed me. How am I supposed to ever trust you again? How do I know you're not going to contact my wife again?"

"That's all you care about isn't it? Protecting your precious little wife."

"We don't have to do this shit at all, me and you. I'm real tired of you throwing my wife in my face, like you didn't know the deal when I met you," he said sharply. "Hear me and hear me good Angelina. I'm not leaving my wife for you. Not now, not ever. So, you can either fall in line, or you can keep it moving. The choice is yours."

"You treat me like I'm not shit. I can either fall in line or keep it moving? This is how you talk to me?" She cut her eyes at him, her face red and her nostrils flared. "Now, after two years you want to say you're not leaving your wife?"

"You heard what I said."

"And what about Andrea? She can keep it moving too, right?"

"If you keep this up, yes. I'll say fuck everything. I'm not playing tug a war with you over Andrea. Whenever we're at odds you want to threaten me by saying you'll take her away from me. I'm sick of that shit!"

Andre didn't mean what he said about walking away from the baby but he was tired of Angelina using her as a pawn. He didn't like to feel like anyone had any power over him. She told him way too many times she would disappear with Andrea, so he was calling her bluff. It was about taking back his control and letting her know that even though she had his one and only child, he still called the shots.

"This is not fair to me Andre," she said, teary eyed.

"My wife could say the same thing," he said sarcastically.

"When you talk like that, it makes me feel like you don't care about my feelings at all," she sobbed.

"You're trying to make me out to be some sort of bad guy, when all I've ever done was be there for you."

"I know you have but still, it doesn't change the fact that I'm left feeling like some side hoe. If you would've just kept it real with me in the beginning I wouldn't be in this situation."

"I told you from day one I was married."

"But you also told me you were divorcing her."

"Look, I'm sorry that I hurt you. But I need for you to understand she was here before you and I love her. She's my wife. If you can accept that, then we can continue doing us like we been doing."

She hated hearing those words come out of Andre's mouth. It was like a knife to the chest. In that moment, reality had finally set in. He wasn't going to leave his wife. She would either have to leave him and move on, or stay and accept things for what they were. Angelina talked a good game whenever she got upset but the truth was, she was nowhere near ready to throw in the towel.

"What about me? Do you love me Andre?"

"That's a stupid question."

She just stood there in silence with her arms folded, waiting for him to answer her question.

"Of course I love you."

"If you love me then I need you to try a little harder. It can't always be about her."

"What do you mean?"

"I need at least three nights a week."

"After everything that just went down, we can't be that bold. Let's take it step by step. Just bear with me, I promise you, it'll get greater later."

"No more broken promises Andre."

He pulled Angelina in close, wrapped his arms around her and kissed her on the forehead. "I gotchu," he said, smoothly.

Angelina looked over at Andrea and noticed she had fallen asleep. She walked over to the play pen, bent down and lifted her out. She draped Andrea over her shoulder and cuddled her closely.

"I heard everything you said, and I'm okay with that but since you're not back at home yet, can you please stay with us tonight?" she asked, her voice soft and vulnerable.

Andre obliged and this softened Angelina right on up. She was weak for him and he knew that. On top of that, she was very easy to control. It was what he liked most about her. Now, all he had to do was fix things with his wife. And he knew that wouldn't be so easy.

The next morning, Andre left straight from Angelina's condo, and drove to the Rolls Royce dealer in La Jolla, which is right outside of San Diego. Andre walked in clean, looking and smelling like money, prepared to spend however much on a "baby I'm sorry" gift for his wife. The salesmen swarmed around him as if they were bees chasing honey.

"Good morning sir, welcome. What brings you in today?" the hungry salesman asked.

"I'm looking for something nice for my wife."

"Is she more of a coupe kind of lady or a sedan?"

"She likes both."

"Follow me," he said, cheerfully. "My name's Brian by the way."

"Andre," he replied as he followed him over to the other side of the showroom.

"This is the new 2016 Phantom Drophead Coupe, from the Zenith Collection. This here is a limited edition. It has a 12 cylinder engine, displaces 6.75 liters and produces 453 horsepower."

"Nice!" Andre exclaimed.

"She's a timeless beauty," he said smiling. "Top of the line. It doesn't get any better than this."

"How much is it going for?"

"485,000, sir."

"I'll take it," he said, without hesitation.

"Okay," Brian replied, as his face lit up.

After Andre closed the deal on the car, he went into work to attend an important board meeting. At Global Consulting business was better than ever. It was now one of the fastest growing consulting firms in the United States. Andre planned on leaving after his meeting and taking off for the rest of the day, however things didn't go as planned. He ended up being swamped at the office, following up with potential clients and overseeing projects.

Later that night, Andre was back at Angelina's again. After making love for the second time, he went into the bathroom and got into the shower. As soon as Angelina heard the water on, she immediately ran downstairs. She remembered he forgot to lock his laptop, and it was the first time in a long time Andre had even brought his laptop inside with him. He usually kept it in the car, but being as though Andre had finally slipped up, Angelina couldn't pass up the opportunity to do a little snooping.

Angelina clicked out of his business documents, and quickly scoped through his home screen. She opened multiple folders, looking for pictures or videos, but there was none. Just a bunch of business files and documents. She tried talking herself out of looking any further, but the urge was way too strong. Why she kept searching for what could potentially hurt her, she didn't know. She just kept saying to herself, *I better not find anything, I better not find anything.* But when she went into his email, what she found completely threw her to the left. One particular email from a woman named Jessica Davis stuck out like a sore thumb, because the subject line read, *last night was amazing.* Angelina frantically clicked on the email thread and scrolled through, reading as much as she could.

Hey baby,

I can't stop thinking about you and all the many times you made me cum last night. My pussy is throbbing right now just thinking about it. I can't wait to feel your dick inside of me again.

Yours Always,

Jessi

Hey handsome,

Are we still meeting tonight? Let me know.

Jessi

There were too many messages to get through and she knew it was only a matter of time before Andre got out of the shower and came looking for her, since she was no longer in bed where he'd left her. She went back to his inbox and continued scrolling down to see what else she could find, as if the messages she'd seen from Jessica weren't hurtful enough. She opened another thread of emails from a woman named, Daniella Sanchez.

Andre,

My husband didn't leave today as planned, so I have to cancel tonight. I promise you, I'll make it up to you when I see you papi.

Daniella

Angelina didn't stop there, she kept scrolling though the emails, only to find more devastating messages. There were too many women, and some of the emails dated back a year ago, which hurt her even more. Her heart was in her stomach, as she continued scrolling. She was afraid of what she'd might see next.

Hey!

It's booked. Room 703. I'm going to fuck you, make love to you, then fuck you again…oh and here's some motivation. See you tonight baby!

Patricia

Looking at the picture Patricia attached to her email, lying on the bed with her legs spread, exposing her bald pink pussy, broke Angelina up inside. She had enough. She slammed the laptop shut and stormed upstairs with tears streaming down her face. Andre was standing in the bathroom, drying off with a towel, when Angelina barged in.

"You're a fucking dog Andre!" she spat.

He looked shocked. "What the hell are you talking about?"

"I'm talking about the emails I just saw. All the nasty little bitches you've been fucking!"

"You went through my computer Angelina?"

"You damn right I did, you nasty son of a bitch! You really are a piece of shit, you know that."

"I'm getting sick and tired of your ass! I've had enough of your drama! I'm done!" he shouted.

Andre went into the bedroom, walked over to the dresser and grabbed a pair of fresh boxers from the drawer. Angelina followed behind him.

"You think I give a fuck about you being done!"

"Cool, glad we're on the same page," he said calmly.

His nonchalant attitude only infuriated her even more. "I'm going to make you pay! I'm putting your no good ass on child support!"

"Do what you have to do."

"How many are there? How many women are you fucking?" she screamed at him, but he didn't answer.

Andre was involved with many women. Unlike most men, he was able to mask his infidelities well. He was very particular with whom he got involved with. All of the women Andre had affairs with were either married, or women in high positions, such as lawyers and judges, women who had just as much to lose as he did. This is how he was able to get away with cheating for so long. Maryana never expected a thing.

She shoved him. "How many?"

"What you fail to understand is that I take care of you! You don't take care of me! Who do you think you are? First, you call my wife and start a bunch of shit. Now, you're going through my emails…naw…I'm cool," he said, leaving out of the bedroom.

Angelina followed him downstairs. "Fuck you! You think because you take care of me, you can treat me any kind of way? I don't need you Andre."

"I guess you don't need me now. You got your meal ticket…right? You knew what you were doing getting pregnant."

"Meal ticket!" Angelina balled up her fist and swung at his face with all her strength.

Andre caught her arm and said, "Calm the fuck down!"

She yanked away and swung at him again. This time her punch landed. Andre had never hit a woman before, but by reflex he backhand slapped her so hard, she fell onto the floor.

Angelina quickly got up and pounced on him like a wild animal, swinging punches and yelling, "I hate you!

Andre grabbed both of her arms in an effort to restrain her and shook her. "If you put your hands on me again, you're going to regret it," he said, in a hateful voice.

Angelina could tell by the fire in his eyes that he meant every word. She had never seen him like this before. She stopped swinging and broke down crying again.

"Get all of your shit out of here and just leave," she said, referring to the boxers, t-shirts, and toiletries that he kept there. "I'm done, I can't take any more of this."

Andre proceeded to walk towards the door. "Throw it out, throw it all out." He turned around and looked at her one last time before he opened the door and said, "you say you're done, make sure you stick to it this time." The door slammed shut behind him as he left. Angelina slid down the wall crying hysterically, terrified that this time it might truly be over.

CHAPTER NINE

It had now been a week and a half since I found out about Andre's affair with Angelina. It still hurt like hell, but I was no longer feeling like a victim and crying myself to sleep every night. I was finally getting to a place where I was pulling myself together. Andre and I still hadn't talked or seen each other, but now I was more than ready to do so. Seeing my mother put a lot of things into perspective for me. She was right, I had to face my problems head on. It was impossible for me to run away from the situation. Andre had a child with this woman and there was nothing I could do to change that. And since I still wanted my husband, we would have to figure this mess out.

I was home doing nothing, bored out of my mind when I got a call from Bree. She said, "get dressed, we're going out." She just met a guy name Sammy who played for the San Diego Chargers. They had only been talking for about a week, and so far so good. Sammy and a few of his teammates were having an all-white boat party, so he told Bree to come through with a friend.

"I'm about to hurry up and get dressed, then I'm coming to your house."

"Why are you coming all the way over here? You don't want to meet up at the dock?"

"Girl Bye. I'm not pulling up in my little ass Jetta."

I laughed. "Okay, crazy. I'll see you soon."

"Alright bye."

"Bye."

I went into my closet and found the perfect white dress, which hugged every curve of my body. It was short, tight, and backless, and the fabric in the front crisscrossed perfectly over my perky 38 D cup breast. My makeup was flawless thanks to Bree. She taught me how to beat my face to perfection. I unwrapped my hair, parted it down the middle and swooped both sides behind my ear. *Now, what shoes am I going to wear?* I thought to myself. *Oooh! I know just the pair*, remembering the white Cruel Summer Giuseppe Zanotti heels I purchased a couple of weeks ago. Bree texted me, *I'm pulling up*. I checked myself out in the mirror again and I was looking good. *Andre is a fucking fool*, I said to myself, admiring my body. I touched up my lipstick, grabbed my YSL clutch, and headed downstairs.

"Hey boo!" Bree said, as she reached out her arms to hug me.

I hugged her back. "Hey bestie! You look sooo cute. I love this dress!"

"Thank you! I love yours too," she said, smiling. She was wearing a very sexy white lace dress that gave off the nude illusion.

"Thanks girl. Which car are we driving?"

"I don't know, maybe the Ferrari."

"Yesss bitch, we're gonna shut it down," Bree said with a giggle and slapping me a high five.

We walked through the kitchen and out to the garage. "I need to get in the gym with you and do some squats so I can get an ass like yours," Bree said, as we walked to the car.

"I keep telling you to come to the gym and stop playing."

"Yeah, either that or I'm getting surgery! I'm tired of walking around with no butt." We both laughed. "Girl, I'm serious I want the kind of ass that'll make a man spend all his damn money!"

"I can't. Something is seriously wrong with you," I laughed.

We pulled up to the parking lot near the dock around 11:30. The lot was packed to full capacity. I could tell by the exotic cars parked in the lot this wasn't some regular party.

All eyes were on us, as we stepped onto the boat looking like two video vixens straight out of a Rick Ross video. I couldn't remember the last time I went out to a party without Andre. I turned down at least five guys within ten minutes of me arriving and I have to admit, it felt kind of good.

"Here he comes," Bree said under her breath.

"Who?" I asked, cutting my eyes, without turning my head.

"Sammy," she murmured. "How do I look?"

"You look beautiful. Aww look at you all nervous," I teased.

Sammy walked up and gave Bree a hug and a kiss on the cheek.

"Sammy, this is my best friend Maryana. Maryana, Sammy."

"I'm just Sammy. No title yet, but I'm working on it," he said jokingly.

He puts his hand out for me to shake. "Nice to meet you."

"Nice to meet you as well," I said.

"Come on, I want to introduce ya'll to my friends," he said, grabbing Bree's hand.

Sammy introduced us to all his friends, which seemed like the entire football team. There was so many of them and most of them were fine as hell. One of his friends handed Bree and I a bottle of Belaire Rose and said, "Turn up!" Nicki Minaj and Beyonce's, "Feeling Myself" came on and we both instantly got hype, holding onto our bottles as we danced closely, winding our asses. "Changed the game with that digital drop. Know where you was when that digital popped. I stopped the world. Male or female, it make no difference. I stop the world, world stop...carry on." The party was lit. Everyone was up on their feet dancing. Bree and I drank and danced all night. It was the most fun I had in a long time.

It was around 11:00 a.m. when I got a call from Andre. I was up but still lying in bed, worn out from the night before. The party went on all night and into the wee hours of the morning. I lost count of how many drinks Bree and I had. All I know is that I was pretty hungover and the sound of my phone ringing annoyingly loud made my head hurt.

I tried to gather myself before answering the phone. I didn't want Andre to think I was lying in bed, still stressing over him. I sat up and cleared my throat before answering. "Hello," I said.

"Hey. How are you?"

"I'm good." I didn't bother asking him how he was doing, because quite frankly I didn't care.

"I know you're tired of hearing me say that I'm sorry but I am. What I've done to you was wrong on so many levels and I'll spend the rest of my life making it up to you."

"I haven't seen you in almost two weeks. In my mind, I'm thinking that you're with her and…"

He cut me off. "I haven't seen that girl. I've been staying at the house," he said, telling half of the truth. "I tried to give you some space after everything happened, but I've been missing you like crazy. I came by the house a few times last week and you weren't there."

I didn't say anything. I just held the phone and let him talk.

"Mary, you're the only one that matters to me. I love you, and I don't want to lose you."

"What about her Andre? How do I know you're not going to keep seeing her?"

"She's not important. She doesn't matter to me. You matter to me," he said in a soft voice. "I need you Maryana, without you, I'm nothing."

"Listen Andre, I would be lying if I said I didn't still love you. I'm just not sure we can get past this. I don't think you understand how deep you hurt me."

"I do understand, and I'm not asking for you to forgive me right now. It's going to take time. And

I'm prepared for that. I'm willing to do whatever it takes to help you get past this."

"I need for us to sit down with her, and I need to hear you tell her that it's over. That's step number one. Without that I can't even consider working on this marriage."

"Done," he said without hesitation. "And to show you that I'm serious. Anything concerning Andrea, it will have to come through you."

"I'm not ready for all that yet."

"I mean later on down the line. Whenever you're ready. I just want you involved, so you're comfortable, that's all."

"Okay."

"Can I come home?"

I took a deep sigh, trying to get a hold of my emotions. I felt conflicted inside. I wanted to curse him out and still be angry, but then another part of me wanted him to just hold me in his arms and tell me everything was going to be okay. He was still my husband, and we took vows before God. Some might say it all went to hell when he stepped outside of our marriage, but in my eyes it was still worth fighting for. However, I wasn't ready to let Andre know that just yet.

"I don't know if that's such a good idea right now."

"Can I at least see you? I won't stay. I just need to see you," he said.

"Okay, fine."

"Thank you."

"Uh-huh," I murmured.

"I have something for you."

"What is it?"

"It's a surprise. Go outside and look out the front door."

"Andre just tell me what it is. I'm not dressed, and besides I'm not in the mood for any surprises," I said in a monotone voice.

He paused. "I want you to see it for yourself."

"Okay Andre."

I pushed the covers off of me and got out of bed, with my head still pounding. I walked over to the bathroom, grabbed my silk robe off the door handle and wrapped it around myself. I grabbed a pair of slippers out of the closet, put them on and headed downstairs. Andre held the phone in silence.

"I'm going out front now," I said.

"Okay."

I opened the door and saw a white Rolls-Royce Phantom Coupe parked in the driveway.

"Oh wow, it's beautiful," I said, as I walked outside.

"It's yours," he said. "Just a little something to show you how much I love and appreciate you."

I opened the driver's side door and sat down on the plush leather seat. I could smell the freshness of the leather. I could tell by the shiny dashboard, and that unmistakable new car scent that this car was straight off the showroom floor.

"It's really nice," I said, admiring the luxurious upholstery. "Thank you."

"You're welcome baby. I'm glad you like it," he said. "Okay, I won't hold you up. I hope you have a good day. Take your new car out for a spin. The keys are in the glove compartment. I'll see you around 6 o'clock."

"Okay, I'll see you then."

"I love you."

"Okay," I said, keeping my guard up. Andre didn't make a big deal out of me not saying "I love you" back. He knew he was still in hot water, and that it was going to take much more than a new car to smooth things over with me.

I had no intentions on divorcing Andre. Like I said before, why should she win? I put way too much time in, sacrificed way too much just to let some woman come along and take what was rightfully mine. When I first found out about the baby I felt as though she had already won or that she had something over me, because she had my husband's only child. Once I sat back and analyzed the situation I realized she was the one getting the short end of the stick. She had his baby, but still so desperately wanted to be in my shoes. She wanted the ring and to be living in the big mansion, waking up to Andre every morning, living together as a family. How ironic, she wanted what I had and I wanted what she had.

Later on that night, Andre pulled up at exactly 6 o'clock. It didn't surprise me because he was always punctual like that. Always on time, not one minute early and not one minute late. He walked through the door looking like a tall glass of water on a scorching hot day. He knew what he was doing walking in looking that good. Hell, I made sure I was looking extra good for him too. I knew Andre loved it when I wore my hair up and off my face, so I pulled it up in a high Chinese bun. I put on a peach Maxi dress and intentionally didn't wear any panties, so that my ass jiggled as I walked. Just a little reminder, in case he forgot that I wasn't some regular, average bitch. I was still young, bad and in my prime.

I didn't know how I would feel when I saw him, or what I'd do. Was I going to see him and get mad all over again? Slap him, curse him out and tell him to leave? To my surprise, I had done the complete opposite. I was still upset and very disappointed in Andre but when he put his arms around me, I didn't want him to let go.

"You look beautiful," he said.

"Thank you," I said, trying my hardest not to crack a smile.

"Can we sit down and talk?"

"Sure."

We walked into the dining room and sat down at the table. He looked nervous, almost childlike, sitting hunched over, staring at the floor, with his hands folded in his lap. He sat like that for at least a minute before even saying a word. I didn't say anything either. Then he looked up at me and said, "I'm ashamed of what I've done to you." I just sat there and gave him a look like, *yeah you should be ashamed.* "It hurts me that I hurt you. I just hope that one day you can find it in your heart to forgive me."

"Since you've been gone, I've been trying to make sense of everything. Trying to figure out where we went wrong, because I thought we were happy," I said, staring into his eyes. "I mean, was I wrong?"

"Of course we were. It was nothing you did. It was all me. I take full responsibility for everything that happened."

"Well then, why'd you do it?"

"I don't know."

"You don't know," I said, squinting my eyes and frowning my face. "If you don't know why you cheated in the first place, then what's going to stop you from doing it again?"

Andre got up and walked over to me, then dropped down to his knees and put his head in my lap.

"I won't ever cheat on you again Maryana. That's my word." He then looked up at me with tears rolling down his face and said, "please don't leave me. I need you."

In the seven years we were together, I never saw Andre cry. When I looked into his eyes I could tell that he was truly sorry for what he'd done. In that moment, the wall I had up came tumbling down. I wrapped my left arm around his neck placed my right hand on his head and gently rubbed his hair.

"I'm not leaving you Andre. I just need some time right now."

He put his arms around my waist. "I love you so much," he said.

"I love you too and there's nothing in the world that can change that. It's going to take some work but we'll get through this. I just need you to be patient with me."

"I'll give you all the time you need," he said, sounding somewhat relieved.

I felt relieved too that we'd finally seen each other and talked about everything in person. I no longer had that negative feeling hovering around me constantly. It would be no walk in the park but I was confident that in time we could repair our marriage. Even still, I planned on making some major changes. No more being the subservient little housewife tucked away in a mansion, high up in the hills. I was going to get out of Andre's shadows, get more into myself and create a lane of my own.

As soon as Andre left I immediately called Bree. I was dying to talk to her, so I could give her the update. She was all for me working things out with Andre. Even when I first told her about Angelina she said, "don't let some thirsty bitch break up your home. If you leave, leave because you want to." Bree agreed that I should take my time and let Andre work his way back in, but what she didn't agree with was, us living apart while we sorted things through.

"I mean ultimately it's your decision to make but girl, if it were me, and I just found out my husband was cheating, the last thing I would be doing is giving him space to cheat again."

"If a man wants to cheat, he's going to find a way to cheat, whether you're giving him little space or not," I said, slightly irritated.

"I guess you're right."

"He came home and laid next to me every night and he still was fucking around, so what difference does it make?"

"You have a point there," she said. "But aren't you worried, just a little bit that he'll slip up again if you push him away too much?"

"I'm not pushing him away. I just told him I need a little bit of time. That's all. I'll let him come home when the time is right, and right now, it's not the time."

"I understand boo, at the end of the day you have to do what's best for you."

"And that's exactly what I'm going to do," I said.

That night I slept like a baby for the first time in almost two weeks. Andre called me before he went to bed just to tell me that he was thinking about me. I thought it was sweet. It reminded me of when we first met. I woke up the next morning to a text from him that read *Good morning beautiful. I hope you have a good day.* I texted back *Good morning. Thanks, I hope you have a great day as well.* I got up, showered and then quickly dressed. I put on a pair of Nike shorts, a matching sports bra and my favorite pair of running sneakers. I plugged my headphones into my cellphone, placed it in my armband and then strapped it on. I ran up the hill for one mile, and then back down for another. As soon as I turned the corner I noticed someone parked in my driveway. At first glance it looked as though it was an unmarked van, but as I got closer I was able to see the words *House of Stemms* printed on the side door panels. I also saw a short and stocky, grey haired man standing at my front door with a clipboard in his hand.

I removed my headphones. "Hello, can I help you with something?"

"Yes, I have a delivery for a Mrs. Maryana Derou."

I laughed to myself because I never changed my last name but Andre didn't acknowledge my last name as Mendez, since the day we got married. "Yes, that's me."

"I have a delivery for you. I just need you to sign right here."

I signed my name on the signature line, placed the pen back in the holder and handed the clipboard back to him.

"I'll be right back," he said.

I turned the key in the lock and opened the door. The delivery man went to the van. Seconds later he returned with seven dozen red roses. I took them from him with a huge smile on my face. "Thank you," I said.

"You're welcome Mrs. Derou. Have a great day," he said, then turned and walked away. I went inside and closed the door behind me. I smelled the flowers, then pulled the envelope from the bouquet and removed the card. It read *7 dozen roses for the 7 wonderful years you gave me. I look forward to many more. Love, Andre.* I went into the kitchen and grabbed an oversized vase, filled it halfway with water, placed the flowers inside and then sat them in the center of my dining room table. I was headed upstairs to get out of my sweaty clothes, and into the shower, when my cell phone started ringing. *It's probably Andre, calling to see if I got the flowers* I thought. But I was wrong. *What the fuck does she want now?* I said out loud when I saw Angelina's number flashing across the screen of my IPhone. I answered fast.

"Hello."

"Maryana, can you talk right now? Are you alone?"

I could tell by the tone of her voice that she'd been crying. "Why? What do you want?" I sighed.

"I need to talk to you." She paused. "Is Andre there with you?"

"About what?" I said with an attitude.

She broke down crying. "I don't even know why I'm calling you with this. Andre and I got into a huge fight the other night," she said, hardly able to finish her sentences.

"Yeah, why are you telling me this? Because your little plan didn't work?"

"Andre wasn't just cheating on you with me. He's been sleeping with lots of women," she cried.

"What are you talking about?" I could feel my heart racing, and my hands weren't steady, they were visibly shaking. I wanted to hang up, but I couldn't. I nervously held the phone, and waited to hear what she was going to say next.

"I went searching through his laptop while he was in the shower...and."

"In the shower?" I said, raising my voice. *This bitch*! I thought to myself. "You're still fucking him?"

"Maryana, listen."

"No. Are you still fucking him?" I repeated.

She paused for a few seconds. "Yes." Before I could even get another word in, she started crying hysterically.

"But's it's over. We're done," she cried. "I'm truly sorry for everything."

"Don't give me that sorry shit. You're not sorry. Didn't you hop back on his dick just the other day? And you have the nerve to tell me that now you're done because you found out you weren't his only side bitch!" I spat.

"You have every right to hate me."

"Hate you?" I laughed sarcastically. "You don't have that kind of power to make me hate you."

"Well maybe you don't hate me but I know you're upset, and I get it. I'm not calling to argue with you."

"I'm still trying to figure out why you're calling. I mean, I don't get you. You did what you set out to do, which was ruin my marriage, and now you're calling to tell me that my husband is cheating on us. Like, seriously, who does this kind of shit?"

"I am sorry whether you believe it or not. It was never my intention to hurt you. I just got tired of Andre messing with my head. He was always lying and trying to manipulate me."

I listened hard. It was somewhat difficult to hear what she was saying through all of the crying. I wanted to stay angry though. I wanted her to be confrontational, so I could go in some more and make her feel even lower than she already felt. But she didn't. Instead, she cried and poured her heart out to me about my lying, no good ass husband.

"Can we talk in person?" she asked, sniffling now. "You can come here, to my house. I just want us to talk face to face and lay everything out on the table."

As far as I was concerned, everything had already been laid out on the table. The fact that Andre could go back and have dealings with this woman after I found out about her, only showed me that he believed he was never in any real danger of losing me. It also showed me that he didn't respect me, or our marriage. I thought about the tears he cried, how I wrapped my arms around him and told him everything would be okay. The thought of me even considering giving him another chance made me sick to my stomach. Andre was a fraud, a liar, and a cheat, who only cared about himself. I knew I wouldn't be able to get past his betrayal. Andre and I were done. But still, I wanted to get next to Angelina. I was curious about her. I needed to see where and how she lived. I wanted to know her…I wanted to see what Andre saw in her.

"Sure. We can talk in person," I said.

"Can you come today?" she said, desperately.

"Yeah, I can come now if you want."

"Okay. I'll text you my address."

"Okay."

Angelina texted me her address immediately after we hung up. I jumped in the shower, quickly dressed and hopped into the new Rolls Royce my cheating husband bought me, and drove over to his mistress's house. I pulled into the entrance to the condominiums where Angelina lived. I entered her house code into the keypad and waited for her to answer.

"Is that you Maryana?"

"It's me."

The panel buzzed and the twenty foot iron gate swung open. I proceeded through the gate and drove slowly through the community, looking for Angelina's house. It was early in the day but it was quiet and peaceful. I could tell it was a nice place to live. I pulled into Angelina's driveway, and parked behind her Porsche Panamera. I got out of the car, walked up to her front door and rang the bell.

The minute Angelina came to the door I could see that she was a wreck. She looked the way I did, when I was down and out, nearly losing my mind. Although I could see pain written all over her face, she was still drop dead gorgeous to me. I mean, she was beautiful. She had these tight almond shaped eyes, thick lips, butter pecan, smooth skin tone, and a body out of this world. She was small, but like me, she was thick in all the right places.

We walked into the house and Angelina closed the door behind us. I could tell by the level of her condo, the expensive furniture and the Porsche parked out in the driveway, Andre had been playing his part with Angelina very well. This infuriated me. *The nerve of him!* I thought to myself. *How dare he take care of another bitch like this? Low down dirty dog!*

"Do you want something to drink?" she asked.

"No I'm okay," I said.

There was an awkward pause, then she said, "I appreciate you coming," as she sat down on the couch.

I sat down next to her but I didn't say anything right away. I just nodded my head in reply. There was another awkward silence. "Where's the baby?"

"She's with my aunt."

"Oh ok," I said. "So what did you find on Andre's laptop?"

"I went into his email and found numerous messages from various women. Some of them were even married." I shook my head in disgust, as she continued. "There were naked pictures, women telling him how good the sex was the night before, all sorts of shit."

Angelina grabbed her cellphone off the coffee table, and started looking through it. About thirty seconds later, she handed it to me and said, "Look at this." She had taken pictures of the message threads with her cellphone. I didn't read every single message. I only skimmed through. When I saw the message that read *I can't get wet for my husband unless I imagine it's you that's fucking me,* I was done.

"What's worse is that there were emails from women that dated way back before he and I even met.

But get this…he said I was the first woman he'd ever cheated on you with."

"He's a beautiful liar honey. He has a way of making you believe every single word he says."

"When we first met, he told me ya'll were getting a divorce but that we still had to be discreet because if you found out about me then you would use it against him in court."

"Wow," I said, in disbelief. "We were never on the verge of getting a divorce. Not ever."

"I know that now," she said, in a low voice.

"So, what happened after you seen the emails?"

"I confronted him about it, and to my surprise he didn't deny it. He started talking crazy, saying he can do whatever he wants because he takes care of me. That's when I just went off. We were arguing back and forth, next thing I know I hit him. Then he hit me back. After that I told him I was done and to get out."

I tried to keep my composure as I listened to Angelina go on and on about the confrontation she had with my husband. Just knowing they were that emotionally involved sent me to a place I had never been before. Inside I was on fire. What was her problem? How could she think it was okay to talk to me about all of this? Did she really think I was her fucking friend or something? I wanted to grab her by the hair, throw her to the floor, and let out all the anger building up inside of me. But I couldn't do that. Not if I wanted my plan to work.

"He hit you?" I said, trying to play it cool.

"Yup. He sure did."

"I guess that's another side of him I don't know." I quickly changed the subject. "You never told me how you two met."

She stood up. "You sure you don't want anything to drink?" she asked. "I'm going to pour me a glass of wine."

"I'll have a glass of wine," I said. I followed her into the kitchen and sat down on the bar stool and watched her while she poured our drinks.

"Andre and I met at a parking garage downtown. He was standing behind me, waiting to pay, but the machine had taken my money and didn't print out a receipt. He told me the machine always did that whenever you used cash."

"Mmm-hmm," I murmured.

"He pulled out his credit card, and paid for my parking, and from there we just started talking."

Angelina went on to tell me how she believed Andre took advantage of the fact that she didn't really have anyone she could depend on other than him. She had just moved to San Diego from Austin, Texas when they met. She was working as a bartender at night and going to culinary art school during the day. She told Andre all about her dreams of wanting to become a big-time chef. He told her that she could do anything she put her mind to and that as long as she had him he would make sure she achieved that and more. Andre even told her that once she was established, he would invest in her so she could open her own restaurant. Now, this really blew me away. Here he was, supporting his side bitch, all the while telling me it's not a good idea for me to go back to work and fulfill my passion as a television news anchor.

Angelina told me she had been on her own since she was sixteen years old. Her mom was a junkie, and like me she had never met her father. She grew up in foster care, jumping from one dysfunctional family to the next. With little to no guidance, she went through life having to figure things out on her own. The little bit of family she had back home, she never talked to. She felt as though they weren't there for her when she needed them the most. Angelina connected with her aunt Sharon, via Facebook at the age of twenty-one. She was living with her husband in Coronado, a city right outside of San Diego. It was because of her aunt that Angelina left Texas, and moved to San Diego. Thanks to Andre she didn't have to sleep on Sharon's sofa for very long. After only two months, he moved her into an apartment and bought her a car. A year later, he bought her the condo she was now staying in.

Angelina cell phone started ringing in the middle of our conversation. She walked back in the living room and picked the phone up off the coffee table.

"Oh my god! It's him! This is him calling me now!" she said, loudly.

"Andre?"

"Yes! What should I do?"

"Answer it. I won't say anything," I said, trying to disguise my anger. "Put it on speaker."

Angelina picked up the phone and pressed the speaker button. "Hello," she said.

"Are you still mad at me?" he asked, in a smooth voice.

"What do you want?"

"I wanted to tell you that I'm sorry about the other day."

"You're not sorry Andre."

"I am…and I miss you."

Angelina didn't say anything back but I got the feeling that if I weren't there, she definitely would have. I moved closer to her so that I could hear him more clearly. Angelina looked as though she was nervous. Maybe she thought I would blurt something out and reveal to Andre that I was there with her.

"I want to see you." He paused for a few seconds. "Is that okay?"

I could tell by the look in her eyes she wanted to say yes. She wasn't going anywhere. Andre had her mind.

"I don't want to see you right now Andre."

"Well, I'm coming anyway. I'll be over there after work," he said firmly, and then he hung up.

Thinking he had me where he wanted me, Andre was now trying to smooth things over with his mistress. After seeing the look in Angelina's eyes when she talked to Andre on the phone, it was clear to me that he had a hold on her. She would never leave him. And now that I saw Andre for who he truly was, I knew he would never be faithful to me. What he was doing to me felt like a crime but unlike before, I didn't feel an ounce of sadness. My heart was now filled with anger and all I wanted was revenge. There was no way in hell I was going to let Andre get away with what he had done to me. Oh, hell no! He was going to pay for the crimes committed against me… and he was going to pay with his life.

CHAPTER TEN

My mind was made up. I decided that I was going to kill Andre. I didn't know exactly when I was going to do it but I knew it had to be done. There was nothing else that could calm the storm that was brewing inside of me. For seven years, I devoted all of me to a man that I didn't even know. I took care of him mind, body and soul. I was a damn good wife. He had the best of both worlds. I was able to hold the house down and keep it sexy for him on the regular. I was his personal chef, housekeeper, stripper and porn star. There was nothing I wouldn't do for him or to him in the bedroom. I would've gone as far as having a threesome with him if he'd asked. Anything to please my husband, but with men like Andre, they're never satisfied. No matter how much of a good woman you are, no matter how pretty you are or how often you please them in the bedroom…they will always be on the prowl looking for their next thrill.

I put my plan in motion. From this day forward, all of my moves were calculated, but in order for things to go as planned, I would have to keep Angelina close. Moreover, Andre would have to stay in the dark about everything. He couldn't know that I'd seen her again, nor could he know that Angelina told me about all the other women he'd been sleeping with. I needed him to believe we were okay, leaving the past behind, and working towards repairing our marriage. See, I was covering all of my bases. If Andre had known that Angelina told me about the women, then nine times out of ten, he would go venting to someone about it. More than likely, it would be his no good best friend, Devin. The last thing I needed was for anyone to suspect I was angry enough to kill him.

I was certain that Angelina wouldn't tell Andre that she'd gone behind his back and contacted me again. Oh, no, she would never do that. She was too much in love with my husband to risk him being done with her forever. So, I knew she would make all of this way too easy for me. On a scale of 1to10 the anger I felt was at 100. I wanted to just get it over with, take a gun, put it to his temple, and blow his fucking brains out, but isn't that how most people get caught? I would have to be very strategic about this if I was going to get away with the perfect murder.

I called Eve and told her I wanted to meet up with her for lunch. The last time we saw each other I was crying on her shoulder like a baby about what her son had done to me. I was distraught and clearly falling apart, not knowing what my next move would be. I needed to see Eve so I could let her know that Andre and I were okay.

I pulled up to this posh Italian restaurant in a downtown neighborhood, nicknamed "Little Italy." I valet parked my Rolls Royce, and tipped the valet parking attendant a fifty dollar bill, and walked inside the restaurant. I reached into my Chanel bag and grabbed my cellphone to call Eve.

"Hello."

"Hey, I'm here. Where are you sitting?"

"I'm outside, on the deck."

"Oh, okay. Here I come."

Eve's face lit up when she saw me walking towards her. With a big smile on my face, I stuffed my cellphone back into my bag and made my way to her table. Eve stood up and put her arms around me and gave me a hug. She looked beautiful as always, wearing a stylish all-white pants suit. The pants were wide legged, but hugged her hips. The three quarter sleeve blazer was open, showing her royal blue blouse, which matched her royal blue Hermes Birkin Bag. Her pants hung long, so I couldn't see what kind of shoes she was wearing but I'm sure they were probably from her favorite, Jimmy Choo.

Eve stood up and put her arms around me and gave me a hug. "Hey beautiful."

"Hey mom," I said, hugging her back.

We both sat down at the table. "How's everything with you?" she asked.

I removed my sunglasses and propped them on top of my head. "Better," I said smiling. "I've decided to go back to work."

"Really? Good for you!" she exclaimed. "News broadcasting?"

"Yup. I've been in contact with my old boss at Fox Channel 5 about coming back and if all goes well at my interview next week, I'll be on the air!"

"That's wonderful. I know that's what you've always wanted."

"Yup, ever since I was a little girl."

"You're going to nail your interview, and you're going to get that job, you hear? You have to claim it. Speak it into existence."

I loved Eve for her good energy. She was always so positive and uplifting in any situation. She was the kind of person that saw the glass as half full and not half empty.

"You're right mom. You're absolutely right."

"How are things with you and Andre?"

"That's what I wanted to talk to you about," I said, before I was interrupted by our waitress.

"Can I get you ladies something to drink?"

"Yes, I'll have a lemonade," I replied.

"I'll have the same," Eve added.

"Okay. Would you like a minute to look over the menu, or are you guys ready?"

We're ready," Eve said slowly, while looking at me to see if I was in agreeance.

"What can I get you?" the waitress said delightfully.

"I'll have the gnocchi with spinach and chicken."

"Okay. Soup or salad?"

"Minestrone soup please."

The waitress then turned to me. "And for you?"

"I'll have the baked ziti with spinach and zeal. And also the antipasto salad."

The waitress confirmed our orders, then said she'd be back with our drinks.

"I've decided to work things out with Andre," I said, with the most sincere look on my face.

Eve started smiling from ear to ear. "I'm so happy to hear that."

"Remember when I asked if you ever thought about leaving your husband?" She nodded. "You said, his bad never outweighed his good."

"Right."

"That's how I feel about Andre. I mean, don't get me wrong, what he did was terrible. But when I think about our marriage and what he's been to me for the past seven years I know it's worth fighting for."

"I would've been by your side whichever way you decided to go but I couldn't be happier to hear this."

The waitress returned back with our drinks, sat them on the table and said our food would be out shortly.

"At the end of the day, I love him and I'm not leaving him for nothing or no one," I said. "I can't let her come between what we've been building for the past seven years."

"Let me tell you something, I don't know that woman Andre was fooling around with, but I know her kind. Women like her intentionally go after successful married men, looking for a come up," Eve said, taking a sip of her lemonade. "She won't be the last to try him either but he has to be smarter than that."

"You're absolutely right, I have faith in him though. I have faith that he'll never do that to me again. I think he'll leave me before he hurts me like that again."

"I hope you're right baby," she said. "I talked with Andre and he still hasn't admitted that he has a child with that woman."

"What did he say?"

"He said he did have dealings with her before but that it wasn't anything serious. Then I asked him about the baby and he said that it wasn't his."

The fact that Andre was still lying about everything, and trying to down play his relationship with Angelina really irritated me. *Ugh!* I thought to myself. *I can't wait to get rid of his ass.*

"The baby is his mom," I said, calmly, trying to hide my frustration. "He told me that himself."

"Did he ever have a DNA test?"

"I don't know but the way that he talked about the baby, it sounded as though he was certain she was his. He discussed taking things to court so that he wouldn't have to go through her. He even said that from now on, he would prefer if I handled everything pertaining to the baby."

"And how do you feel about that?"

"I think Andre wants me to feel comfortable about everything and for me to know he's not still seeing her," I said. "I think it's probably best we handle things that way."

"I agree," she said, nodding her head. "I'm sure Angelina won't be too happy about that."

"She's already pissed off now that Andre broke things off with her. She called and texted my phone so much, I had to put her in call block," I lied.

Eve's eyes widened, her eyebrows went up, and her jaw dropped. "Noooo," she said.

"Mom, I'm telling you, that girl is crazy. Like, obsessed with him." I paused for a moment, giving her chance to take in what I'd just said. "But you know what, Andre now sees her for what she is and he wants nothing to do with her. We're leaving her right where she belongs…in the past."

Eve and I continued talking over lunch for the next hour or so. I was intentionally spilling the tea, and she was taking it all in like a sponge, hanging on my every word, as I told her half-truths. Eve couldn't stand Angelina and she'd never even met her. She didn't trust her either. Her exact words to me were, "you make sure you keep an eye on that damn Angelina." Little did she know, I was the one Angelina should've been keeping an eye on.

The very next day, I went to a local electronics store, and bought a prepaid cell phone. I registered it under a bogus name, Christina Walker, and I made sure to pay in cash. I even went as far as to disguise myself in a blonde bobbed wig, hat, glasses and a fake pregnant belly, in which I made out of foam. Even before I was plotting Andre's murder I had never dialed Angelina's number, not even once, and now it was imperative that I keep it that way.

I walked out of the store and around the corner where I parked my car. I hit unlock on my key fob, got into my car and started the ignition. I removed the phone I had just bought from its box, and pressed the power on button. I then grabbed my cellphone out of my bag and pulled up Angelina's number, then I dialed it from the pre-paid phone.

"Hello," she answered.

"Hey. It's me, Maryana."

"Oh, hey. You changed your number?"

"Yeah, I did this morning."

"I called you last night."

"I was knocked out when you called," I lied. "But what's going on? Did you need to talk to me about something?"

"I did last night but I'm over it now. Besides, I know you're tired of hearing about all of this."

"What happened?" I asked, pretending to be concerned.

"Another argument with Andre," she said in a low voice. "Now all of a sudden he wants to go to court to establish paternity and then petition for partial custody."

"Oh yea," I said casually. "He talked to me about that."

"What did he say?"

"From now on, he wants to go through the courts regarding the baby," I said, adding fuel to the fire.

There was silence on the other end of the phone.

"Hello," I said.

"I'm here," she replied in a sad voice. "I hate him, I swear."

Yeah, sure you do bitch, I said to myself. I quickly snapped back into focus. "Trust me, I understand. Well, I'm actually not far from you right now. I can stop by if you want to talk."

"Sure, thanks. Come on over," she replied.

I removed my disguise, stuffed everything into a plastic bag and tossed it in the backseat. I put my car in drive and quickly sped off down the busy street, and onto the highway. After about fifteen minutes of driving, I arrived at Angelina's house. She greeted me at the door, holding Andrea in her arms.

"Come in," she said.

Angelina closed the door behind us then I followed her into the living room, where we sat on the sofa. Andrea was sitting on her lap, cooing and chewing on a teething ring.

"Hi there," I said, gently touching the side of her cheek. She looked at me with my husband's eyes and smiled.

As much as I despised both Angelina and Andre, I didn't have any ill feelings towards the baby. She was innocent in all of this. It wasn't her fault she had two fucked up parents.

"Somebody's teething, I see."

"Say, yes I am. I'm cranky too," Angelina said, in a baby voice, as she patted her on the back.

"Aww poor baby," I said.

Angelina walked into the dining area, and put Andrea in her walker.

"Can I use your bathroom?" I asked, putting my handbag over my shoulder.

"Sure. It's upstairs, to your left."

I intentionally walked pass the bathroom, and continued walking straight. To my right, in the middle of the hallway, there was Andrea's room, fit for a princess. The walls were painted a soft pink and all the furnishings were white. Her crib wasn't just any regular crib. It was a convertible crib with an elegant diamond tufted upholstered headboard attached. Right above her crib there was a crown embedded in the wall, with a sheer pink canopy hanging from it. And the carpet; it was the kind of plush carpet that your feet sink into and leave footprints.

I left Andrea's room, and walked further down the hallway. There was another room on my right.

Although it was beautifully decorated, I could tell it wasn't Angelina's bedroom. It felt cold. I figured it had to be a guest room or something. So, I left out, opened the door to my left and there was the master bedroom. It was decorated elegantly and expensively, much like my bedroom at home. As a matter of fact, her entire house gave me a familiar feeling. I knew Andre had a lot to do with that. Luckily I was wearing flats that day. Otherwise Angelina would hear my heels click clacking against her hardwood floors, since Andrea's room was the only one carpeted. As I stood there in Angelina's room staring at her bed, my mind drifted off. Thoughts of them lying closely together, while he whispered, "I love you" in her ear and thoughts of him making passionate love to her spiraled through my mind. I could see Andre behind her, thrusting in and out of her from behind, pulling her hair and smacking her ass. I could feel the anger bubbling up inside of me again. I hurried out of Angelina's room, down the hall and into the bathroom. I turned on the faucet and splashed cold water on my face, but it didn't help slow down my racing heart. *Only a little while longer* I thought to myself as I looked at my flushed face in the mirror. *Just a little while longer.*

I gathered myself and went back downstairs. Angelina was in the kitchen fixing Andrea a bottle. I sat down on the sofa, and waited for her to return. Andrea was still in her walker, banging against the walls and furniture, as she circled around the house. I noticed that she'd left her cellphone on the arm of the sofa. I picked it up and pressed the home button to see if there was a passcode on it. There wasn't, so I slid my finger to the right to unlock. My hands were shaking. I didn't have enough time to go through messages. At this point, I didn't care what Andre had been texting her anyways. I knew they were still fucking, so it didn't really make a difference. I composed three messages, sent them to myself and then quickly deleted the message thread from Angelina's phone.

Angelina took Andrea out of her walker, and placed her in a playpen with her bottle. She laid Andrea down on her side and propped a pillow underneath her head. Andrea put the bottle into her hands, to her lips and began anxiously feeding herself.

"So, what are you going to do about all that court stuff?"

"I guess I don't really have a choice but to go along with it."

"If you think about it, it's probably better for you anyway."

"Why do you say that?"

"After paternity is established, he'll be ordered to pay a set amount of child support each month."

"But the fact that he even wants a DNA test just pisses me off."

"That's how men are. They'll switch up on you like that," I said, snapping my finger. "At this point, you have to do what's best for you and the baby."

"You're right," she said, in a soft tone.

"When's the last time you seen him?"

"Umm…"

I knew a lie was coming.

"I haven't seen him since the last time we got into that huge fight," she said, in a not so convincing voice.

"What about that night he said he was coming over? He didn't come?"

"Nope."

I knew she was lying, I just didn't care. I acted as though I believed her and continued listening to her tell me about how she was done with him and ready to move on with her life.

"Andre can't be trusted. Look at what he did to me. And now what he's doing to you. He even had the audacity to say to me that if I take him back, he'll stay away from Andrea."

"He said that?" She now looked serious and almost breathless.

"Mmm-hmm. That's when I knew he wasn't shit," I said. "Look when I first found out about you, was I angry? Hell yes. But I realized the only person I should be mad at, is him. He betrayed me, not you. You don't owe me anything." She just sat there, listening and nodding as I talked. "At the end of the day, I know he hurt you too. All I'm saying is, be smart. Look out for you and your baby, because at any given time Andre can say fuck you and Andrea. Then what? You're gonna have to drag his ass to court anyway. So, you might as well get it over with now."

She nodded her head to everything I said "You're absolutely right."

"And now he's talking partial custody? Girl puh-lease. He got some nerve. Go get a lawyer fast."

"You know what? That's exactly what I'm going to do. I'll show his ass," she said, with a deep grin on her face.

A week had passed and now everything was set in place. Like a game of chess, I managed to strategically play both Angelina and Andre, all the while setting up for the kill. I visited Angelina at her house a few more times, and I talked with her almost every day, making sure that I stayed in her head enough to where she would continue to be at odds with Andre. He and I saw each other every day but I made it clear that I wasn't ready for him to come home. I told him with tears in my eyes, "I want us to get back to the way we were and the only way we're going to do that, is to take our time and work on it." He believed me, even agreed to see a marriage counselor. He said, "I'll do whatever it takes to get us back to where we were before."

Mrs. Blanchard called me and asked if I could speak at her charity event. It was short notice but hosting was like second nature to me, and besides, attending her event with hundreds of people would give me the perfect alibi. "Of course. I would love to," I said. "I'll be sure to bring my husband as well." "Wonderful," she replied. "I'll see you love birds tomorrow at eight."

It was around 5:00 p.m. when I started to prepare for my last date with my husband. While showering, I thought long and hard about what I was about to do. It brought me pleasure rather than fear. Not one time did I ask myself, are you sure you want to do this? There was no doubt in my mind that I would go through with it. I was anxious and ready to get it over with. I pulled two dresses out of my closet. One was red, the other was white, and still wrapped in plastic. I grabbed a pair of never worn nude sling back heels from Christian Louboutin, and placed them on the floor, next to the bed. Wearing only my bra and panties, I sat down at my vanity mirror to do my hair and makeup. I pulled my hair to the back in a slick bun. I usually preferred a natural, no-makeup look but this night in particular, I went dramatic. I put on my favorite red lipstick by Chanel, puckering my lips and then smoothing the lipstick by rubbing my top and bottom lip together. I then smiled at myself in the mirror. I pulled my diamond chandelier earrings out of the jewelry box and put them in my ear. They were a gift from Andre for our fifth year anniversary. I got up from the vanity and then walked over to the bed where my dresses lay. I picked up the red dress, stepped into it, and carefully slid it over my curvaceous hips. I sat down on the edge of the bed and put my heels on. I grabbed my Lolita Lempicka perfume off the vanity and sprayed my neck and wrist. It was Andre's favorite. I then went back to my closet and searched through my large collection of handbags and clutches, until I found a nude Hermes clutch that matched perfectly with my heels. I stuffed the clutch inside my large tote, turned off the lights, and left out. I walked downstairs with my other dress draped over my left arm, and my handbag in the other. I pondered at the front door for a minute before opening it. I wanted to make sure I wasn't forgetting anything important. *The wine!* I remembered. I went into the dining room and grabbed a bottle of Pinot Noir from the wine cabinet. *Okay, I've got everything,* I said to myself. I then walked to the front door, and set the alarm before locking up behind me.

"On my roof. Dark and I'm burning a rose. I don't need proof. I'm torn apart, and you know. What you did to me was a crime. Cold case love. And I let you reach me one more time, but that's enough." Rihanna's "Cold Case Love" blasted through the speakers of my Rolls Royce. I kept repeating the song over and over, feeling every single word and thinking about what Andre had done to me. I thought about how even after I found out about Angelina, he still didn't end the affair. Even with all the other women he was sleeping with, he didn't love me deep enough to end it with the one woman that came between us and caused me so much hurt and pain. He wasn't sorry for what he'd done to me. But at this point, I'm like fuck it. You don't have to feel remorse, compassion or even an ounce of sadness, but one thing's for sure…you will feel my wrath.

I arrived at Andre's house a little after 6:00 p.m. The block was so quiet I could hear crickets. It was hot, but breezy and I could hear the wind whistling in the trees. As I got out of the car, and walked to Andre's front door I felt my heart racing. I wasn't afraid though. I think it was all the anticipation that was making me nervous. I took a deep breath, exhaled slowly and rang the doorbell. The minute I saw Andre's face, all the nervousness went away. With my game face on, I wrapped my arms around him and kissed him passionately on the lips. He grabbed the bottle of wine out of my hand, walked into the dining room and sat it down on the table. I followed behind him.

"Damn! You looking good!" he said, checking me out.

"Thanks baby," I said, with a smile.

"And you're wearing that perfume I like."

"I sure am."

Andre wrapped his arms around my waist and pulled me in close to him. He squeezed my ass and kissed me again. "Damn I've missed you."

"You just seen me yesterday silly," I said.

"Naw. I mean, I miss you, miss you."

"How much?" I said, licking my lips.

He took my hand and put it on his crotch, and I felt his dick, hard as a rock through his pants.

"Down boy," I giggled. "We've got all night. Why don't you go put on some music, and I'll pour us a glass of wine."

"That sounds like a good idea."

I walked into the kitchen, and grabbed two wine glasses from the cabinet. I opened my clutch and grabbed one of the three vials of Nembutal I brought with me. I filled Andre's glass halfway with wine, and the other with the Nembutal. I took a spoon and stirred quickly, then rinsed the spoon off and put it back in place. I put the empty vial back into my clutch, and then poured me a glass of wine.

"Hey girl, ain't no mystery, at least as far as I can see. I want to keep you here lying next to me, sharing our love between the sheets. Ooooh oooh baby, baby, I feel your love surrounding me…"

I walked into the living room, and over to Andre and handed him the glass of wine.

"Let me find out you're trying to seduce me," I said jokingly. "You just had to throw on that good ol' Isley Brothers huh?"

"You know how I do," he said, staring at me with those deep brown eyes that once captivated me. "Remember when we first met, and you tried to play hard to get?"

I laughed. "Oh, shut up. I was not playing hard to get. I couldn't stand your cocky ass."

Andre popped his collar. "I still got you though right?

"Whatever," I said, smiling.

"No, but in all seriousness, from the moment I laid eyes on you, I knew you would be my wife. I said to myself, with a woman like that by my side, there's nothing I can't accomplish." He took a long sip of his wine. Inside I was nervous, hoping that it wouldn't taste funny. "It was like God made you especially for me."

Oh, puh-lease, I thought to myself. *So you could do me dirty! Lie to me, cheat on me and treat me like shit! I don't fucking think so!* I forced a smile to hide my annoyance, then kissed him on the cheek. "We were made for each other," I said.

I grabbed his hand and walked over to the sofa. I didn't want him standing too long, and then suddenly feel dizzy. I needed him to sit, relax and drink as much as possible. I put my hand on his thigh and began rubbing it slowly. "You know I'll never leave you right? No matter what comes our way. No matter how tough it gets…I'll never leave."

"I know that baby, I know," he said, in a smooth tone. "You're my ride or die."

"And I always will be." I saw that Andre had finished his drink, so I took the empty glass from him, went into the kitchen and filled the glass to the rim. This time I put twice as much Nembutal as I did before.

"Here you go baby," I said, handing him the glass of wine.

I sat close to him and began massaging his neck and shoulders. He closed his eyes, dropped his head forward and sighed. "That feels so good," he said.

"Finish your drink daddy, I'm about to make you feel real good," I said seductively. Andre sat up straight, and took another big sip of wine.

"Oh yea?"

"You know I am," I said, before finishing my drink. Andre tossed his back too and I knew that it was only a matter of time before his body shut down. A lethal dose of Nembutal is between 5-10 milliliters. Andre consumed 20 mililiters.

"I never told you this before, but I never felt as though I belonged to anyone, until you came along. Coming from where I'm from, growing up the way I did, you were like a breath of fresh air to me."

Andre put his hand on his chest, and swallowed hard. He then made a grunting noise as if he was trying to clear his throat. I stopped massaging him, and turned him to me, so I could look him in the eye.

"I held you high on a pedestal. I used to think you were the answer to my prayers. Like, you saved me or something." I chuckled sarcastically. "But now, you know what I think of you? I think you're a piece of shit. You're a dog Andre. A low down dirty dog, but you know what? Every dog has its day, and well today…it's your day muthafucka!"

Andre eyes looked as though they were going to pop out of its socket. He stood up slowly, his knees buckled but he still tried to make his way into the kitchen. "What the fuck is going on? What…did…you…do…to…me?" He was now slurring his words.

"What did I do to you? No, it's what you did to me!" I said, my voice thick with emotion. "We had it all Andre. We had a good life. I was a good wife to you. There was nothing I wouldn't do for you. I loved you with every part of me. And what do I get in return Andre? Huh? What do I get in return? Lies! And betrayal! That's what I get!"

He opened his mouth, gasping for air, as he dropped to his knees. "Maryana…please," he said, before falling flat on the floor.

I shook my head in disgust. "You fucked up Andre," I said in a strangely calm voice. Angelina told me everything. I know you were still seeing her. She told me about all the other women too."

I stood over top of him, staring him down with fire in my eyes, until he took his last and final breath. "Good bye Andre, you should've known better than to cross me."

I stepped over Andre's lifeless body and went into the kitchen, searching for something I could use to clean things up a bit. First I opened my handbag, and grabbed the plastic gloves I packed. I put them on and then opened the drawer and found a microfiber cloth. I wiped my fingerprints from everything that I had touched, including the wine bottle. I went into the living room and did the same. I took any evidence with me that would've placed me at the crime scene, and I got out of there.

I got into my car, and drove off. It was now 7:20 p.m. and I had to be at Mrs. Blanchard's event by 8:00. My mind was racing, as I sped down the road and onto the interstate. I kept replaying everything over and over, retracing my steps in my head, making sure I didn't leave anything there that would incriminate me. *I'm good. Everything is going to be alright.* I pulled over at a quiet corner in a residential neighborhood, and I put my car in park. I checked out my surroundings and there wasn't a person in sight. I quickly got out of my red dress, and slipped into the white one. I made sure my hair was in place, and touched up my makeup. I removed the clutch from my handbag, and transferred all of my necessities; credit cards, driver's license, makeup etc. I then stuffed my red dress inside my handbag and put it on the backseat floor.

I strutted into the ballroom, with a smile on my face, greeting guest, as if it were my own party. I was calm and at ease, as though nothing happened...like I didn't just kill my husband less than an hour ago. I texted Andre's phone, *Honey, where are you? We're about to start.* Just as I was putting my phone away, I felt a tap on my shoulder. I turned around and it was Mrs. Blanchard.

"You look lovely darling."

"Thank you, so do you," I said. She gave me a hug and a kiss on the cheek. "Where's Andre?"

"I'm waiting on him now. He should be here shortly. The place looks great. Do you need me to do anything before we get started?"

"Oh, no dear. Thanks, but all I need for you to do is get out there and do what you do best. Get them all to pull out their check books and wallets." She winked at me and smiled, before walking away.

The event was a success. The donation amounts received were larger than anticipated, and Mrs. Blanchard was ecstatic about it. She said she owed it all to me, and that I had the gift of the gab. Throughout the party, I was sure to call Andre a few times. I even sent another text, *I can't believe you didn't show. Everyone here is asking where you are and I don't even know what to say. Don't even bother coming now. It's damn near over.*

I needed to make one stop on my way home. I drove down interstate 15, and exited off the highway. I parked off to the side near an overpass, got out of the car, walked onto Lake Hodges Bridge and threw my pre-paid cellphone into the lake. I walked back to my car with an overpowering feeling of solace. I finally got the revenge that I so desperately needed.

The next afternoon, at approximately 12:30 p.m. my doorbell rang. I opened the door to find two police officers standing on my doorstep. "Are you Mrs. Derou?" one of the officers asked.

"Yes," I replied, with a confused look on my face.

"I'm Officer Pierce and this here is Officer Gray, and we're with the San Diego Police Department. May we come in?"

I nodded yes, after both officers flashed me their badges.

"What's going on?"

"You might want to sit down," Officer Gray said.

I'd rather not. Can one of you please just tell me what's going on?"

Officer Pierce looked me in the eye and said, "I'm sorry to inform you ma'am, there's been an accident involving your husband."

"Accident? What accident? Is he okay?"

"I'm sorry ma'am," he said, sympathetically. "I'm afraid, he's dead."

"No, no, he's not dead. He can't be. He's not dead." Like an actress on cue, I burst into tears. "Nooo it's not true," I sobbed, dropping to the floor.

Officer Gray picked me up from the floor, and walked me over to the sofa. I continued to cry hysterically. After at least five minutes of carrying on with the dramatics, I calmed down. "What happened to my husband?"

"He was found dead of an apparent heart attack," Officer Pierce said.

"Heart attack? How is that even possible? My husband was the healthiest person I know."

"The post-mortem examinations show that he died of heart-failure."

"This doesn't make sense," I said, with tears still rolling down my cheeks. "Where was he found?"

"You have a second residence correct? 15888 Hardwick Lane?"

"My husband sold that home years ago."

Both officers looked at each other with a perplexed expression, then Officer Gray turned to me and said, "No, ma'am, your husband was found there this morning, lying on the dining room floor."

"What? By who?"

The officer pulled out a small notepad from his back pocket and flipped it open. "Devin Towns."

"That's his best friend," I said, in a low voice, looking down at the floor. "Wow. I had no idea he kept the house."

"I'm sorry ma'am."

"Where's my husband's body?"

"He's at UC hospital's morgue. Arrangements need to be made so that he can be transported to the morgue or funeral home of your choice."

"Okay officer," I said, standing up. "I have to get there."

"Are you okay to drive?"

"Yes, I'll be fine." My voice is now hoarse and raspy from all the crying. "Thank you officers."

When the officers left I immediately called Andre's mother. Her cellphone went directly to voice mail. I called the landline, and didn't get an answer. I quickly left out of the house, jumped into my car and rushed over to see her. When I pulled into her driveway I instantly became nervous. I knew looking Eve in the eye and telling her Andre was no longer here would be extremely hard for me to do, especially since I was the one responsible for his death. I was worried she would be able to see right through me. *You can do this Maryana…no one knows you had anything to do with this. You got this*, I said to myself, as I walked to the door, and rang the doorbell.

"Hey mom, I tried calling you."

"I was out in the garden baby. Come in," she said.

I walked in and she closed the door behind me. Before I said anything else I thought about what Andre had done to me. I thought about the pain I felt when I learned of his betrayal. I needed to go back to that place emotionally so that I could cry when I broke the news to her. "The police just left my house." I took a long and dramatic pause. "They informed me that Andre's dead." Tears streamed down my face as I uttered the words.

Eve's face went blank. "What are you talking about dead?"

"He died from a heart attack," I said, in a sad tone.

"Heart attack!?" she said, raising her voice. "I just seen Andre two days ago. He was in perfect health. My baby didn't die of a heart attack."

"I know. That's exactly what I said, when the police told me. Something is off. Something just isn't right."

"What are you saying Maryana?"

"We have to get over to the hospital. We'll talk about it in the car."

Eve grabbed her purse and before you could blink, we were out the door. While in the car and on our way to the hospital, she called Andre's father and told him the news. To my surprise Eve didn't break down. She didn't cry a single tear. Maybe she was in denial about it all.

"Now, talk to me. What do you mean something isn't right?" she quizzed.

"Andre was supposed to meet me last night. I hosted an event for a friend of ours and he never showed. We were supposed to go together, but around 4 o'clock he called me and said he would meet me there."

"Mmm-hmm," she said, staring at me as I drove.

With both hands on the steering wheel I glanced at her periodically. "Eight o' clock came and he wasn't there. Now, you know that's not like him."

"Right. He's never late," she said.

"Exactly. Well, anyways, I called and texted. No response. I went home, called and texted again. Nothing. To be honest with you, I thought he was doing something he had no business doing. Like maybe he was with Angelina or something."

"Mmm-hmm."

"Then today the cops show up at my front door telling me that my husband died of a heart attack. And to my surprise, the officer told me that Andre was found at the house on Hardwick Lane. Mom, I thought he sold that house years ago."

Eve was silent and listening hard to every word I said. Good thing I hadn't opened my mouth to anyone about the house when I found out from Angelina. As far as everyone was concerned I didn't find out that Andre kept the house until the day the police showed up at my door.

"So did I. He never sold the house?" Eve asked inquisitively.

"The officer said that's where Devin found him, lying on the dining room floor. I can almost bet Angelina knew about that house too," I said firmly. "And there's something else you don't know."

"What's that?"

"When Andre cut her off, she started losing her mind. She sent me threatening messages telling me that we both were going to pay and that he fucked with the wrong one. Then to make matters worse, Andre filed for partial custody. Angelina was livid."

"Oh, Maryana, why didn't you tell me all of this sooner?"

"Remember the day we had lunch I mentioned to you that she called and texted me so much I had to put her in call block? I even told you I thought she was crazy."

"Yeah, I remember."

"I just thought Andre and I had it under control."

"Do you think she had something to do with Andre's death?"

"Well, first off, you and I both know he didn't die of a heart attack. Second, Andre cuts her off and within a week he turns up dead? Come on mom…what do you think?"

I had Eve right where I wanted her. She was convinced that Angelina had something to do with Andre's death, so I knew she would make the rest of my plan fall into place way too easily.

When Eve and I got to the hospital Andre's father was already there. He looked at us with sad eyes, and his face wore the same expression. I could tell by looking at him that he'd already seen what we were about to see. He held our hands as he walked us into the hospital morgue where all the lifeless bodies lay in rows. The room was cold, still and had the smell of death. The morgue attendant walked us to a cold sterile metal table where Andre's body lay under a white sheet. He pulled the sheet back to Andre's waistline and then stepped back, so we could have a closer look. The moment Eve saw Andre's bloodless face and stiff body she started bawling. Kenneth stood beside her and held her in his arms as she cried hysterically. "No!" she sobbed. No!"

I ran out of the room, and back out to the hallway, and dropped to my knees in tears. "Why God why?" I cried.

Eve and Kenneth came out to the hallway, to find me losing it. Kenneth picked me up off the floor and wrapped his arms around me, telling me it's going to be okay.

"It's not going to be okay. It's never going to be okay. My husband is gone. He's gone," I sobbed, playing the role of the grieving wife exceptionally well. All of a sudden I hear the sound of heels clicking down the hallway. We all turn to see a woman dressed in a black pants suit walking in our direction. Eve, Kenneth and I stood closely as she approached us.

"Are you the family of Mr. Andre Derou?"

"Yes. This is Andre's wife, and we're his parents," Kenneth said.

She shook his hand. "My name is detective Meshach," she said, in a thick Russian accent. She flashed her badge to us all, and then turned to me and said, "I have a couple of questions for you."

"Sure," I said, choking back a sob.

"When is the last time you saw your husband alive?"

"Yesterday morning."

"Around what time?"

"Eleven or so."

"I have reason to believe that Andre wasn't alone last night when he died. Any idea who might've been there with him?"

"I do actually."

"Who?"

I put my hand over my mouth and broke down in tears again.

"That bitch, Angelina! That's who! She killed him! And I want to see her pay for what she's done to my son!" Eve said, with a menacing scowl on her face.

"My husband died of no heart attack," I added. "We want an autopsy done."

"We've ordered one Mrs. Derou. Trust me, I want to find out what happened to your husband just as much as you do."

Kenneth put his arm around his wife, as tears rolled down her cheeks. Seeing how upset Eve was getting, he turned to the detective and said, "this isn't a good time detective. Can we do this another time?"

"Fair enough. Why don't you guys come down to the station tomorrow so we can discuss this further?" Detective Meshach says. Then she reached into the breast pocket of her white blouse, pulled out a business card and handed it to me. "Here take my card." I took the card from her and agreed to come down to the station. The three of us left the hospital shortly after the detective left. Kenneth said I was in no shape to drive and insisted I leave my car at the hospital and ride home with them. As much as I wanted to go home, and just be to myself, I did as he said. When we got to the house I called Bree frantically and told her about what happened. She left work and came over immediately. Yes, Bree was my best friend and I trusted her more than anyone in the world but I couldn't tell her the truth about what I'd done. Funny thing though, if I had told her, I could imagine her looking me square in the eye and saying, "Fuck em', he deserved it." Still, it was a gamble and I damn sure wasn't about to risk my freedom. So, I continued playing the same role with her as I did with everyone else. Everyone was taking it hard, especially his brother Jackson. He sat on the sofa, in silence staring at the wall. Their phone was ringing off the hook, and I could hear his mother repeating over and over that Andre was dead. Then to make matters worse I overheard Devin talking to Kenneth about how he found Andre dead. It was time for me to go. Seeing everyone so distraught was weighing on me heavily. I couldn't wait to be out of that house. I hugged and kissed his mom and told her I would call her, and I left. Bree drove me to the hospital to get my car, then she followed me home and stayed the night with me.

The next morning Andre's body was transported to the morgue, where the toxicologist would perform an autopsy. Bree drove me to the police station so I could meet with Detective Meshach. I walked into the police station knowing exactly what I was going to say. Eve already put the bug in Meshach's ear that Andre had been murdered, by Angelina and now all I had to do was prove that she did have reason for wanting Andre dead.

Detective Meshach came to get me from the waiting area. "Mrs. Derou, follow me this way, please."

I stood up, turned to Bree and said, "I'll be right back."

I followed Meshach down the hall and into a small room with one wooden table, and two chairs. "Would you like a cup of coffee?" she asked, pulling out a chair for me to sit down.

"No, thank you."

"Water?"

"No, I'm okay. Thanks."

She sat across from me at the table with a notepad, pen and cup of coffee in front of her.

"Mrs. Derou, how long were you and Andre married?"

"We were married for six years and together for seven."

"And how would you describe the marriage? Would you say that it was a happy marriage?"

"Yes, we were very happy. Up until about a month ago I thought we had the perfect marriage."

"What happened a month ago to make you think different?"

"I found out my husband was having an affair."

"And that must've made you angry. Right?"

"Of course it did."

"Your mother in law mentioned a name yesterday…a uh…Angelina. Is this the woman your husband was having an affair with?"

"Yes."

"She seems to think Angelina is responsible for Andre's death. Any idea why?"

"There's been a lot going on within the last couple of weeks."

"I'm listening," she said, in her deep Russian accent.

"I started receiving calls from an anonymous caller. They wouldn't say anything. I mean, they would call all hours of the night. Then one day I get a call from Angelina telling me she's been having an affair with my husband, and that they share a child together."

Detective Meschach jotted something down in her notepad, then took a sip of her coffee, but didn't say anything. She just stared at me with curiosity in her eyes.

"I asked Andre about it and he denied everything. He said it was someone messing with me, you know, just trying to make me upset."

"Did you believe him?"

"No," I said, without hesitation. "I knew she was telling the truth about the affair. However, I wasn't sure about the baby."

"So, then what happened next?"

"She called me again the next day and said she wanted to meet. We met at Bayview Park and…"

"What date and time was that?" she interjected.

"I don't remember the exact date, but it was three Saturdays ago, at 1 o'clock."

She started writing again in her notepad. "Okay," she said. "You can continue."

"When I arrived I saw that she wasn't alone. She had the baby with her, and with just one look, I knew she belonged to my husband. I also recognized Angelina from a party my husband and I had. She showed up and I can remember her just staring at me. She looked angry and I just had a feeling that something was off. I wanted to have a conversation with her but when I went looking for her, she was gone."

"Did Andre see her?"

"I don't know."

"Okay, so, you met in the park…"

"Yeah. We talked and she told me everything I needed to know regarding her relationship with my husband and that was it. I left. I didn't hear from her for a few days, but then she called again when she and Andre got into a huge argument."

"Wait. Let me get this straight. The woman who was having an affair with your husband called you to tell you they had a fight?"

"Yeah, crazy, I know. Well it got even crazier when my husband told her it was over and that he wanted nothing to do with her."

"How so?"

"My husband and I decided we were going to make our marriage work. He was trying to do

151

everything in his power to let me know the affair was over. He even called her in front of me one day and told her we were working things out and that she shouldn't call him unless it concerned the baby."

Detective Meschach leaned forward with her elbows on the table, resting her chin on her hands. "How did she respond to that?"

"She cursed him out, and then Andre hung up on her. A couple days later, he decided he wanted to take Angelina to court to establish paternity, request that he be put on child support, and then file for partial custody."

"Why did he want to do that?"

"So that there would be boundaries. He wanted everything to be handled through the court. Angelina was out of control. She was calling him non-stop. She was even calling me. She started sending me threatening text messages saying, I better sleep with one eye open and that Andre and I were going to pay for screwing her over.

"Do you still have the text messages Angelina sent you?"

"Yeah. I do, actually."

"May I see them?"

I reached into my handbag and grabbed my cellphone. I unlocked my phone, pulled up the text messages and then handed the phone to Detective Meschach.

Are you so desperate that you'll stay with a man that cheated on you and had a baby on you? Andre loves me. I have his child and we're going to be together. I belong with him. Not you. You don't love him the way that I do. And Andre doesn't love you the way that he loves me.

You think you won? Well, think again. Andre still belongs to me bitch. I'm not going anywhere. I have his one and only child. Or did you forget? Silly ass bitch. Tricks are for kids. LMAO

This is all your fault. You think I don't know you're the one putting Andre up to all of this. I'm not going to let you or that lying, two faced, piece of shit you call your husband get away with screwing me over.

You fucked with the wrong one bitch! I'm going to show you just how bad things can get for the both of you. You better sleep with one eye open!

Detective Meshach jotted down Angelina's phone number and then handed my phone back to me.

"You must've been pretty upset about all of this right? You learn your husband's not only having an affair but that he also has a child with the woman."

"Yes, I was upset. I've said that already."

"Whose idea was it to get the life insurance policy?"

"It was my husband's idea. We both took out policies on each other after we were married."

"A million dollars is a lot of money Mrs. Derou. Some might even kill for that amount of money."

"Well, if you've checked our bank accounts then you would know that a million dollars is nothing to me."

"When did you last see your husband?" Meshach asked again, trying to catch me in a lie.

"I told you already. I saw him the morning he died, around 11. Why are you badgering me with this nonsense?"

"I'm trying to figure out exactly what happened to your husband."

"Listen, I didn't kill him, if that's what you're getting at."

"Well, if that's the truth then there shouldn't be a problem giving me a DNA sample."

"I have nothing to hide but what you're implying is absurd. The house where my husband was found, I hadn't stepped foot in that house in years. Andre told me he sold that property. You're wasting time interrogating me when you should be out there trying to find out who did this to my husband," I said, with tears welling up in my eyes. "I loved Andre and nothing in this world could've changed that. Yes, what he did was wrong, but we were working on that. Andre was doing everything he could to make things right between us. I would've never hurt him. Not ever."

Detective Meshach sighed deeply, then looked at me and said, "I'm not accusing you of anything. I'm just trying to get to the bottom of this, that's all. In order for me to do my job I need to make sure I follow proper protocol, and with that being said, Mrs. Derou, where were you last night between the hours of eight and ten."

"I was hosting a charity event at the Royal Hall. Andre was supposed to meet me there, but he didn't show. I called and texted a few times but I didn't get an answer."

"And what time did you arrive and leave the event?"

"I arrived a little before 7:30 and I didn't leave until close to midnight."

"Is there anyone that can corroborate that?"

"Absolutely. Mrs. Blanchard. It was her event."

"Okay, I'll be needing her contact information."

"Of course. Is there anything else?"

"Well, we're finished here. But I would still like to collect a DNA sample."

"Okay, let's get to it then. Like I said, I have nothing to hide."

CHAPTER ELEVEN

Angelina walked into Claremont Funeral Home to attend Andre's viewing, wearing a black dress, black sheer stockings and black heels. Her hair was pulled back in a ponytail and she wore dark shades that were slightly too big for her small face. The moment she walked into the viewing room Maryana spotted her. Seeing Angelina's face at her husband's viewing took her to a familiar place and she didn't like the feeling it gave her. It reminded her of when Angelina overstepped her bounds and showed up at the charity gala. She couldn't believe that Angelina, being Andre's mistress, had the audacity to show up to her husband's viewing.

"There she is. That's Angelina," Maryana said to Eve, pointing in Angelina's direction.

They walked over to Angelina and stopped her dead in her tracks.

"You've got some nerve showing your face here after what you've done," Eve said, her voice heavy with anger.

Angelina thought Eve was referring to the affair. "I'm sorry. I'm not here to cause any trouble."

"You need to leave," Maryana said, firmly.

"What are you talking about? I have every right to be here."

"No, actually you don't! You don't have any rights when it comes to my husband!" Maryana spat.

"You think you're smart don't you? You show up here, and act like you had nothing to do with it. You murdered my son. You bitch!" Eve raised her hand and slapped Angelina hard across the face.

Angelina stood there for a moment in shock, holding her face. "You better be glad I was taught to respect my elders. Otherwise, I'd lay your ass out on this floor."

"I want you out now!" Eve shouted.

"It's time for you to go," Maryana said. "Security!"

"You know what, you're so fucking fake. Fuck your security," Angelina said, before abruptly walking out the door.

Two days after Andre's funeral, Angelina is called down to the police station for questioning, as if she hadn't been interrogated enough by Andre's mother. When she arrived Meshach and her partner Detective Cole took her to a small private room, with one table and three chairs.

"Have a seat," Detective Cole said.

Detective Meshach sits down at the table, and places a large manila folder in front of her, along with a tape recorder. Detective Cole is sitting next to Angelina, while Detective Meshach sits directly across from her and has a stoned expression on her face. She crosses her legs and presses record on the tape recorder.

Detective Meshach states the date and time and then asks Angelina to identify herself.

"Angelina Bonet."

"Now let's start with last Sunday. According to your phone records you called Andre at 3:15, and again at 5:47 p.m."

"I did."

"What was the nature of your conversation?"

"We just talked regularly like we always did."

"Did you two have an argument?"

"No."

"From my understanding, you and Andre were having an affair. Correct?"

"That is correct."

"For how long?"

"About two and a half years."

"Were you two still having an affair when he died?"

"Yes. Andre and I were in love."

"And how did you feel about him being married to another woman?"

Angelina paused to collect her thoughts. "At first it was okay I guess, but then as time went on and my feelings for him grew stronger, I wasn't okay with it."

Detective Cole just sat there quietly next to her, eyeing her like a hawk and reading her body language, while Detective Meshach asked all the questions.

"Had you ever expressed that to him?"

"I have."

"Did he ever tell you he would leave his wife for you?"

"Yes."

"And did it make you angry that he didn't?"

Angelina sighed in annoyance. "What does this have to do with anything? How is any of this relevant?"

"It's our job to determine relevancy," Detective Meshach said, leaning forward, resting her knees on her lap and folding her hands. "Where were you on Sunday night between the hours of eight and ten?"

"I was home, with my six month old daughter," Angelina said with an attitude.

"Is there anyone that can corroborate that?"

"Uh, no. I just said, I was home alone with my daughter."

"So, you have no alibi?"

"Alibi? What is this? Am I under arrest?" she asked, with a look of panic written all over her face.

"You're not under arrest, but I don't think you understand how serious this is. This is a possible homicide. If there's anything you know, then you need to start talking now, because as of right now all signs point to you."

"Bullshit! If all signs point to me then why am I not in handcuffs? I haven't done anything wrong and there's nothing I can tell you because I don't know anything."

"Then help us exclude you as a suspect by giving us a DNA sample."

"You need to be questioning his wife. Not me! She's the one who was angry enough to kill him. What reason would I have for wanting Andre dead?"

"You were in love with a married man. You wanted him for yourself. Andre told you he wasn't going to leave his wife for you, and you snapped."

"You're kidding me right? Now, you're reaching."

"Angelina it's simple, give us a DNA sample, and that will exclude you as a suspect."

"I'm not giving you anything until I consult with a lawyer. Now, if I'm not under arrest I would like to go now." Angelina was furious that the detectives were insinuating that she could possibly have something do with Andre's death. As far as she knew Andre died of a heart attack. She knew she did nothing wrong, therefore, she believed she had nothing to worry about. If she had known what Maryana put her up against, she would've handled things a lot differently.

"You're free to go," Meshach says in a carefree voice.

Without hesitation Angelina stands up, flips her hair and storms out. Cole turns to Meshach and says, "So what do you think?"

"I think she's guilty."

"So do I."

"It's simple. She's having an affair with a married man, who she has a kid with. After two and a half years of being his mistress, she's had enough and wants more. She calls the wife up and exposes the affair, only to have it blow up in her face."

Cole nods. "So she thought his wife would leave, then she could finally have him all to herself, but instead he dumps her."

"Then to make matters worse he tells her he wants partial custody of the baby. She calls him, asks if they can meet so they can talk. Maybe discuss the whole custody battle, or maybe she tries to get him to come back, their little meeting doesn't go as planned. She kills him."

"Only problem with that is that if she acted out of anger and killed him, it would've looked like a crime scene and not staged as an accidental death. If Andre was indeed murdered, it was carefully thought out."

Meshach nods in agreeance. "We're looking at premeditated murder." She grabbed the manila folder and tape recorder off the table, and they both walked out of the interrogation room, and back to their desk. As Meshach sits down, another homicide detective walks over and says, "The wife's alibi checks out. I checked the security footage from the Royal Hall and she was definitely there the entire night. I spoke with Mrs. Blanchard, she said Maryana's behavior didn't seem off at all. In fact, she told me Maryana did a hell of a job hosting her charity event, and that she raised over 100,000 for her that night."

Meshach placed her left thumb under her chin and her left index finger up along the right side of her nose. "And her cellphone records show she did in fact call him multiple times during the event."

"Correct. We also have the text she sent to Andre's phone asking his whereabouts."

"And what about that number? Did we get a trace on the phone number from Angelina's phone records?"

"Yes. It belongs to a Dr. Ernest Shaw, at 7789 Mira Mesa Blvd."

"Why would she need to speak with a doctor so frequently? That number came up at least thirty times this past month."

"Well, she does have an infant."

"So, what does that mean?"

"I forgot you don't have any children. Babies are always sick and when my kid was an infant, I swear my wife called the pediatrician for every little thing. If he had a runny nose, she would freak out."

"I hear you but with that much communication, it has to be more of a personal relationship," she said, getting up from her desk. "Thanks for this." She walked over to Cole and asked him to come along and pay Dr. Ernest Shaw a visit.

Meshach and Cole arrive at 7789 Mira Mesa Blvd, and both looked at each other with raised eyebrows when they find that it's a veterinary clinic. They got out of the car and walked into the clinic, which was very slow and quiet. They were greeted by an older attractive receptionist, whose nametag read *Sharon*. "Good afternoon Sharon," Cole says, while flashing his badge. "I'm Detective Cole, this is my partner Detective Meshach, and we just have a few questions for you."

"Sure. What can I do for you?"

"Do you know a woman by the name of Angelina Bonet?"

"Yes, she's my niece. Is she in some sort of trouble?" she asked in a concerned voice.

"I can't answer that truthfully at the moment. We're investigating the death of Andre Derou, and right now we're following every lead."

"I see."

"Do you have a close relationship with Angelina?" Meshach asked.

"I would think so."

"We haven't been able to locate any of her relatives."

"Oh, yeah well, that's because she doesn't have any."

"What do you mean?"

"She grew up in foster care down in Austin Texas. She reached out to me on a social networking site about four years ago, and three years ago she moved here with me."

"She lived with you?"

"Yes, my husband Ernest and I."

"Dr. Shaw is your husband?"

"Yes," she said, right before the office phone started ringing. "I'm sorry I have to take this."

"Oh, no problem. You've answered all of our questions. Thank you for your time Mrs. Shaw," Meshach says.

"Enjoy the rest of your day." Cole adds.

"Hello, Dr. Shaw's office." Sharon answers, as Meshach and Cole walked away.

Two days after Sharon informed Angelina that two detectives came by the office asking questions about her, Angelina returned back to the police station, with her lawyer to give a DNA sample. She still felt as though she had nothing to worry about, and she truly believed that once Andre's autopsy and toxicology results came back then all of their murder theories would be put to rest. Still, Angelina decided to cooperate with the detectives, that way she'll at least be excluded as a suspect, but little did she know, it was way too late for that.

As the weeks went on Angelina hadn't heard a thing from the detectives. She assumed she was in the clear and that all of their accusations were proven to be invalid. Nevertheless, Meshach and Cole were still working around the clock, building a solid case against her. However, until they had sufficient evidence they were keeping the rest of their investigation under wraps. With all of the drama now behind her, she was now really mourning Andre's death. Losing the father of her child was a tough pill to swallow. She cried many days, and many nights. But every time she looked into her daughter's eyes she was reminded that she still had a part of him, a part of him that not even his wife had. Now, all she wanted was a clean slate. A chance to start a new life, in a new place, far away from San Diego, California.

Detective Meshach is sitting at her cluttered desk, reviewing a case file on a new homicide the chief has just given her. As she flips through the manila folder, reviewing the gruesome details, she's suddenly interrupted when her phone rings.

"Homicide. Detective Meshach speaking."

"It's Brooks, from the lab. We have the results from Mr. Andre Derou's autopsy report."

"What do we have?" she asked eagerly.

"I found traces of Nembutal. With a blood alcohol level of 0.15, the Nembutal was multiplied, causing his heart to go into cardiac arrest."

"Nimutal? Meshach says, mispronouncing, in her heavy accent. "Andre overdosed on Nimutal?"

"It's Nembutal, also known as Pentobarbital. It's a short acting barbiturate that is most commonly used by veterinarians to euthanize animals."

"Veterinarians use this drug to put animals to sleep?" Meshach asked, thinking back to the day she and Cole visited Dr. Ernest Shaw's office.

"That is correct. It was widely used as a sleeping pill or an anti-anxiety drug, but because it's highly lethal in overdose, it was taken off the market."

"How fast does it act?"

"For animals, death occurs within 15-30 seconds of injection. For humans, it can take anywhere from 15 minutes to a couple of hours, but with the high levels of Nembutal and alcohol found in Andre's system, my guess is that he died in a matter of minutes."

"Thanks Brooks, how soon can you get the full report over to me?"

"I'll send it over now."

"Thanks Again."

"You got it."

"We got her," Meshach said, loudly as she hung up the phone. She got up from her desk, turned to Cole and said, "The results from Andre's autopsy report came back. There were traces of Nembutal found, a drug used by veterinarians, to put animals to sleep," she said, putting an emphasis on "veterinarians."

"It's not a coincidence that Angelina's aunt works at a veterinary clinic," Cole says, with a smirk.

"I told you I was right about her."

Meshach gathered her team and informed the Chief they were prepared to make an arrest. "I'll make a call to the judge and get us a warrant," the Chief said. "Good work detective."

It was around 6:00 p.m., when Detective Meshach and Cole arrived at Angelina's residence. Cole knocked on the door, waited for a minute, and then knocked again, but this time his knock was forceful and dominant. "Coming," Angelina shouted. She looked out of the window and saw a black Crown Victoria and two patrol cars out front. She then looked out the peephole, and an uneasy feeling overtook her when she saw the two detectives. Angelina quickly grabbed her cellphone and called her lawyer. "The cops are here, I don't know what to do."

"Open up Angelina, or we're coming in!" Detective Cole said firmly.

"I think they're here to arrest me. I, I, I thought you said I was okay," she stuttered.

The knock at the door grew louder. Thump, thump, thump!

"Angelina open the door and surrender. Don't answer any questions. I'll see you at the station. Don't worry. I'll handle this," her lawyer said.

"Angelina Bonet, you're under arrest. You have the right to remain silent. Anything you say can and will be used against you in a court of law. You have the right to an attorney. If you can't afford an attorney, one will be provided for you. Do you understand the rights I have read to you?" Detective Meschach said, as she slapped the handcuffs on Angelina's wrist.

"My baby! My baby is upstairs! Please let me call someone to get my baby!" Angelina said frantically.

"We'll take care of that," Meshach said, as she walked Angelina to the police car.

"But I haven't done anything! I haven't done anything wrong! I'm innocent!" she cried, as Detective Meshach put her hand on the top of Angelina's head and guided her into the back of the police car.

CHAPTER TWELVE

On September 11, 2015 Angelina was charged with first degree murder. A week later, during her preliminary hearing a judge denied her lawyer's request for bail. The prosecution had motive and a substantial amount of evidence pointing to Angelina as the murderer of my husband. Still, she went against her lawyer's advice and refused to take the plea bargain offered by the prosecutor, whereby she would plead guilty to second degree murder. After pleading not-guilty, Angelina will now have to sit in prison and await a trial, facing twenty-five years to life for a crime she didn't commit.

I know you're probably wondering how I actually pulled it off. Well, I wasn't keeping Angelina close to me for nothing. Once I decided I was going to kill my husband, I also decided I would frame his mistress for the murder. At first I didn't know exactly how I was going to kill Andre, but when Angelina told me about her Aunt, and that she worked at a veterinary in which her husband owned, I thought *Perfect, I'll do it by drug poisoning him.* I went to the library and started researching different drugs that were used by veterinarians. There were way too many. I narrowed my search down to drugs that veterinarians used to put animals to sleep, and there it was, Nembutal. The more I researched the drug I knew it was the perfect drug for me to use to kill Andre. It was fatal, fast acting, and completely painless. I went online and ordered the Nembutal from a company based out of Peru, and paid with a pre-paid debit card. I was sure to register the debit card under a fake name. I knew that once the cops learned of Andre's affair, they would pull all of our phone records. I wanted them to see that Angelina called me in the middle of the night from blocked numbers and the other times after that. This would only help me prove my case that she was harassing me. What I didn't want them to see is constant communication between the two of us, which is why I purchased the pre-paid cellphone. Now all I would have to do was keep her close enough so that I could execute my plan. It was easy, like taking candy from a baby. Each and every time I was at Angelina's house, pretending to be her friend, while listening to her vent about my husband, I was setting her up for his murder. I sent threatening text messages to myself from her phone, then deleted them. One night Angelina and I were drinking and talking. She went upstairs to check on the baby. I quickly grabbed a Kleenex from my handbag and used it to pick up the empty wine glass she'd been drinking from. I then stuffed it into an oversized zip lock bag and put it into my handbag. I went into the kitchen to grab another wine glass for Angelina and poured us both another drink. The very next night, after getting rid of Andre, I swapped my wine glass for the one with Angelina's prints and DNA all over it. So, you see, Angelina's best bet would've been to take the plea deal. No jury in their right mind will believe for a second she's innocent, and the way I see it, she's as guilty as they come. I didn't ask for any of this. I didn't ask for Angelina to come into my life the way she did. She came through like hurricane Floyd, with all intent to destroy. She wanted to destroy a life I worked so hard to build. Just come right in and take my fucking husband, like I didn't even exist, or like marriage held no merit. When I said, "till death do us part," I really meant that.

On this morning, I felt good. You know that feeling when there's finally sunshine after constant rain? Well, that's how I was feeling. I was home cleaning, with my feel good music blasting through the speakers of my 70-inch flat screen TV, when I barely heard my phone ringing. I grabbed the remote control, pressed mute, and then grabbed my phone off the kitchen counter.

"Hello," I answered.

"Hi, Yes, is this Maryana Derou?" I rolled my eyes, at the sound of my deceased husband's last name. It would've come off a bit strange if I'd corrected her and said, *no, my last-name is actually Mendez.* So, I answered, "Yes it is, whose calling?"

"My name is Patricia Conley, and I'm calling from The Department of Children and Families."

"Okay," I said, in a confused voice.

"Is this a good time to talk?"

"Uh, yea. Sure."

"The reason for my call is that we're in the process of trying to find a home for eight-month-old Andrea Derou."

"Find a home for her?" I asked, now, sounding even more confused.

"Apparently her mother doesn't have any living relatives, other than her aunt Sharon Shaw. Andrea was in her care for a couple of weeks but has now informed us that she can no longer care for the child."

"Wow," I said, shocked that Angelina's own blood aunt would turn her back in a situation like this. "So there's no one else?"

"Apparently not. Your late husband is listed as the father and since he's no longer with us, you're considered Andrea's next of kin."

"Okay," I said, waiting for her to finish.

"Would you be able to take on the responsibility of being her legal guardian?"

"Does her mother know about this?"

"Once we find placement, then she'll be notified."

"And what happens to Andrea if I say no?"

"First, we'll contact Andre's side of the family and if we can't find anyone that can take her, then she'll go into foster care."

"I can't let that happen," I said. "I'll take care her."

"Oh, that's wonderful," she said, delightfully. I could sense that she was smiling on the other end of the phone. "You're really doing a good thing here. It makes me feel good knowing there's people like you that exist in this cold world. After everything she's done to you and your family, you're still willing to care for her child and bring her into your home.

"Well, she's innocent in all of this. Besides, it's what my husband would've wanted."

"I commend you for that."

"Thank you."

"Maryana, let me tell you a little about the process."

"Mmm-hmm," I replied.

"Well first, we'll conduct a background check on you, and while we're waiting for that to come back, we'll send someone out to inspect your home to make sure that our home safety checklist guidelines are met, and also that you have enough space for the child."

"Oh, yes, that won't be a problem. I have a seven bedroom home."

"Wonderful," she said. "Do you think you can come down to my office tomorrow to fill out the paperwork?"

"Sure. What's a good time?"

"How's 10 a.m. sound?"

"That works for me."

"Okay, great. Do you have a pen and paper? I'll give you the address."

"Uh, yea. One second," I said, opening the kitchen drawer to find a pen and piece of paper.

"I'm ready."

"The address is 5500 Campus Drive and we're on the fourth floor."

"Got it."

"And please be sure to bring a valid driver's license, and your social security card with you."

"No problem."

"Okay, great. I look forward to seeing you tomorrow," she said.

"Okay. Thanks for calling."

"No, thank you. And Angelina should be thanking you too. She doesn't know how lucky she is. If it weren't for you, her child would more than likely end up in the foster care system."

"We certainly don't want that to happen."

"Oh, gosh no. In the U.S. there are currently over 500,000 children in foster care and more than half of them get lost in the system. But don't get me started. I'll start babbling, and I don't want to hold you anymore than I already have."

I chuckled. "Oh, it's okay. Thanks again for calling and I'll see you tomorrow. 10 o'clock right?"

"Yup that's right."

"Okay. Enjoy the rest of your day."

"You too. Goodbye," she said, pleasantly.

"Bye."

Life is funny, I thought to myself when I hung up the phone with Patricia. I know this might sound kind of strange but I was ecstatic when she called. I wanted a child more than anything. Who would've thought that things would turn out this way? Yes, she was the product of an affair my husband had with his mistress, but she didn't ask to be here. She was innocent. She needed me and I was going to be there for her. I was going to love and protect her as if she was my own child. I could hear Andre's voice in my head, *I feel like Andrea is a blessing to the both of us, since you can't have a child of your own.* At the time, I didn't see the logic in that, but after it's all said and done, after everything I've been through. All the miscarriages, and all the pain it's caused me…I guess he was right after all.

A Month Later…

"Hey bestie!" Bree said, hugging me. She then bent down to kiss Andrea, who was sitting in her stroller. "Hey, angel face!"

"Say, hey Auntie," I said, smiling.

"Ugh, girl it's been forever. It's so good to see you. I was beginning to feel like Celie from The Color Purple."

"Nothing but death can keep me from you," I said, jokingly.

She laughed hard. "I've missed your crazy ass."

"I missed you too girl. I didn't mean to stay away for as long as I did. I just needed to sort things through," I said, pushing Andrea in the stroller as we walked through Fashion Valley Mall.

"No, I completely understand. You've been through a lot these past few months. I'm just glad to see you getting back to yourself."

I sighed. "Tell me about it. I'm still not used to Andre not being here, and I probably won't ever get used to it but one thing for sure is that, I'm getting on with my life."

"Good for you," Bree said, while peeping a beautiful white coat on a mannequin in the window of BCBG Maxazria.

"That's a must have," I said, right before Andrea started fussing.

"Isn't it!" she exclaimed. "Let's go check it out."

Andrea started to fuss some more. "Hang on a minute." I said, sitting down on the bench. I reached into the stroller and began unstrapping her. "Somebody's tired of the stroller already." I lifted her out of the stroller and sat her on my lap. She stopped crying instantly.

Bree sat down next to me, smiled and said, "can I say something to you without you taking it the wrong way?"

"Of course, you can," I said, cuddling Andrea close to me.

"You seem happier now. Just looking at you with her, and seeing you in such good spirits, it makes me happy. The glow I see around you now, I've never seen that before."

"Aww. How could I take that the wrong way?"

"I don't know girl. I just didn't want you to think I meant that you're happier now that Andre's gone or that you were never happy with him, because I know that you were, but it just feels like a different vibe now."

"No, I know what you're saying, and you're right. I am happy, and I haven't felt this way in a really long time."

"You've got what you've always wanted now."

"I know Bree finally. And my mom and I are in a really good place too. We talk all the time now."

"Aww boo, I'm so happy to hear that."

"She's coming to visit next month."

"Oh really? I know she's looking forward to seeing the baby."

"Yeah, she is," I said, looking at Andrea. "She's going to fall in love with her."

"She's so attached to you. And you're so good with her," Bree said.

I smiled. "I'm attached to her too. Look at her, doesn't she have her daddy's eyes?" As I held Andrea in my arms, staring into her pretty brown eyes, I felt complete, like everything was exactly as it was supposed to be.

Nobody knows why people do what they do, but what I do know is that when good people do bad things, it's usually for a reason. I never thought in a million years things would have gone down this way, but you know it's true what they say, there is nothing in this world more dangerous than a woman scorned. Besides, there's just certain situations you can't put a woman like me in. I've been through too much, seen too much, loved too hard, only to have my heart broken by the one person I loved more than anything in the world. The lack of remorse shown by my husband and his lover left me no choice. I mean, what else was I supposed to do? Let them get away with it? I think not! Do I regret what I've done? The answer is no. If I had to do it all over again, I would do it just the same. One day I'll have to pay for what I've done. That's life. The circle of karma never ends…but for now, I have my happy ending.

ABOUT THE AUTHOR

Beverly Sade is an author, actress and entrepreneur. As a former model Beverly has been featured in music videos, magazines, such as Smooth Magazine and Hiphopweekly. She has also appeared on Starz hit television show, "Power," and MTV's "Guycode." In the winter of 2016, she will be making her big screen debut, playing the role of a news reporter, Megan Stone, in the film "But Deliver us From Evil. At an early age Beverly learned that writing was her passion, writing screenplays, short stories and poetry. Beverly's writing has earned her an editor's choice award for outstanding achievement in poetry, presented by The International Library of Poetry. At the age of 21, she wrote "Shadow of a Gold Digger." In 2013, she established Beverly Sade Publications, producing the best-selling novel "The Blame Game." "Hail Mary" is her third.

www.ingramcontent.com/pod-product-compliance
Lightning Source LLC
Chambersburg PA
CBHW070031260626
47159CB00005B/2012